MURDER ON THE ITALIAN RIVIERA

T. A. WILLIAMS

Boldwood

First published in Great Britain in 2024 by Boldwood Books Ltd.

Cover Design by Nick Castle

Cover Photography: Shutterstock

A CIP catalogue record for this book is available from the British Library.

Paperback ISBN 978-1-83518-754-8

Large Print ISBN 978-1-83518-750-0

Hardback ISBN 978-1-83518-749-4

Ebook ISBN 978-1-83518-747-0

Kindle ISBN 978-1-83518-748-7

Audio CD ISBN 978-1-83518-755-5

MP3 CD ISBN 978-1-83518-752-4

Digital audio download ISBN 978-1-83518-746-3

Boldwood Books Ltd
23 Bowerdean Street
London SW6 3TN
www.boldwoodbooks.com

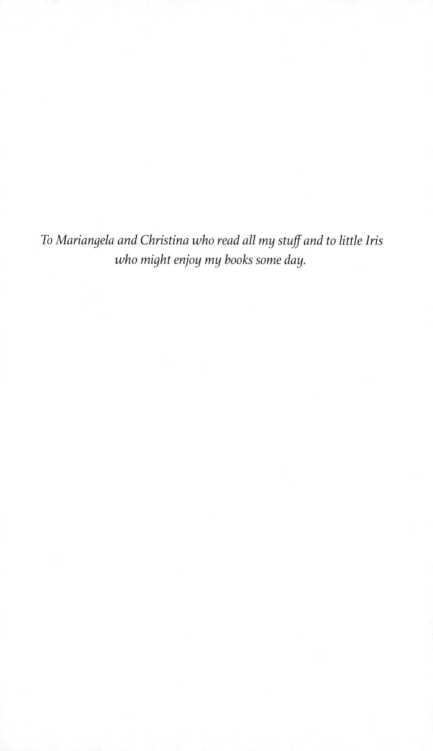

To Mariangela and Christina who read all my stuff and to little Iris who might enjoy my books some day.

1

MONDAY AFTERNOON

'Signora Moretti to see you, Dan.' Lina held the door open for the new client.

I got up from my desk and went across to greet my visitor. She was probably in her mid-thirties, just a bit older than my daughter, and she had close-cropped, dark hair. There were worry lines around her eyes but, even so, when she addressed me, there was a hint of a twinkle in them.

'Do you recognise me, Chief Inspector?' In spite of her Italian surname, she was speaking English with a London accent.

I took a closer look at Signora Moretti and there was definitely something familiar about her face, but my soon-to-be-fifty-seven-year-old memory banks took a few moments to retrieve the name. To give myself a bit of time, I took a chance.

'You've changed your hair since I last saw you.'

She nodded. 'I did that after the first few weeks inside. It's much less fuss like this so I've stuck with it.'

To a former copper like me, her use of the word 'inside' could mean only one thing. Belatedly, my brain coughed up the details.

'It's Bianca, Bianca Moretti, isn't it? Nine months for being an accessory, if I remember right.' It was all coming back to me now. It had been one of my last cases a couple of years ago when I'd still been a DCI in the Metropolitan Police and shortly before I'd opted for early retirement. Moretti had been caught up in the particularly brutal murder of a particularly brutal gangland boss responsible for much of the narcotics trade in South London. His name had been Peter Hasani, the son of Albanian immigrants, and he had been based in Peckham. The murder weapon, a sawn-off shotgun, had been found in her flat with three sets of prints on it, none of them hers. There had been no residue on her hands or clothes and she had denied all knowledge of the weapon or indeed the murder victim, but the judge had found her guilty of obstructing a murder investigation and had jailed her as an accessory.

Fortunately for her, two witnesses had identified the actual killer, the leader of another equally ruthless drug gang in nearby Brixton. He had been a nasty piece of work of southern Italian extraction called Lodovico 'Vico' Carnevale. At the time, his name had been linked to Bianca Moretti – although she had steadfastly denied being in any kind of relationship with him – and we had apprehended him at Gatwick as he had been about to board a flight to the Bahamas. His prints had matched those found on the shotgun and his DNA was on the body. He had been tried and convicted and I assumed he was still safely locked away at His Majesty's pleasure and would remain there for quite a few years to come.

'I'm glad to see your memory's still working, Chief Inspector.'

'Just Dan Armstrong these days, Bianca. I retired a couple of years ago. Like the sign on the door says, I'm a private detective now.' I indicated a couple of chairs by the window, overlooking the little medieval courtyard of this ancient Florentine building.

'Take a seat and tell me what brings you here. I presume you don't just want to reminisce about old times.'

She sat down on one of the chairs and as she did so, there was a creak of wicker and Oscar – realising that my visitor was female – roused himself from dreams of squirrels and food and climbed out of his basket to say hello to the new arrival. Bianca Moretti looked charmed to meet him and reached down to ruffle the Labrador's ears.

'And this must be the famous Oscar.'

I tried to keep the surprise out of my voice. 'I'm sure he's glad his fame precedes him, but how come you know his name? For that matter, how did you know I was here?'

She managed a hint of a grin but I could see she was struggling. Clearly, something was bothering her. 'I read the papers. There was an article about you and your murder mysteries in *The Sunday Times* a couple of months back.' To my surprise, she reached into her bag and pulled out a copy of *Death Amid the Vines*, my first book, which had come out in March and had benefitted enormously from a full-page article in the colour supplement written by a journalist friend of mine. 'I bought it at the airport two weeks ago and I thoroughly enjoyed it.'

'You aren't telling me you came all the way to Florence just to tell me this? Not that I'm not honoured, you understand.'

She set the book on her lap and her expression became more serious. 'No, this isn't the only reason I'm here. I need your help.' Before I could speak, she held up her hand. 'I'm not asking for charity. Money's not a problem. I'll pay whatever you ask.'

It came as no surprise to hear that she had money. In the course of investigating the Hasani murder, we had come across suitcases full of cash, both in his house and in Carnevale's, along with a complex trail of shell companies and offshore bank accounts, no doubt many of which still harboured ill-gotten gains.

'Let's worry about that when we get to it. For now, just tell me what brings you here.'

She appeared to concentrate her attention on Oscar, who was by now happily stretched out on the cool, terracotta floor tiles. It was only the end of May but Florence was already experiencing a heatwave with temperatures around thirty degrees.

'There's been a murder.' She stopped and corrected herself. 'At least, that's what I think, and my father agrees with me.'

'But not everybody thinks so? Aren't the police involved?'

'That's the point – they say it was an accident.'

'And you and your father don't think it was.'

'No, we don't.'

'Would you like to tell me all about it? Where's this happening? In Italy, I presume, or you wouldn't have come to me.'

'Yes, it happened at my pop's campsite. It's in a little village not far from the coast. One of the campers was found dead yesterday morning – a British guy. His body was floating face down in the swimming pool.' Although her tone was deadpan, I could sense an undercurrent of emotion – but dead bodies can do that to people.

'And what makes you and your dad think it was murder? Any signs the victim was assaulted or held underwater? Drugged, maybe?'

She shook her head. 'According to the police, no. They say he'd been drinking heavily. There was a nasty bruise on the back of his head and they say he must have slipped, banged his head and toppled in. The pathologist says death was definitely by drowning, and misadventure was the conclusion, but we're not convinced.'

'Care to tell me why you think otherwise?'

'I really don't know. That's why I've come to you.' If I hadn't already crossed swords with her, I would have accepted this at face value, but a part of me started questioning just how much she did know. Could I trust her or was there something else bubbling away beneath her impassive exterior – like trying to get revenge on me, for example? I decided to give her the benefit of the doubt for now, but I had a feeling I might regret it.

'Would you like me to go and see for myself?'

She answered immediately. 'Definitely. That way, you can see the place for yourself and do your detective thing.'

'Whereabouts on the coast is it?'

'It's on the Italian Riviera coast halfway between Genoa and the French border.'

'I see.'

That was quite a bit further away than I'd been expecting and I did a quick calculation. By car that was probably about four hours away from here, along one of the nastiest stretches of motorway in Italy. The Ligurian coast is very beautiful but famously hilly and rocky, and the motorway, while undeniably a wonderful piece of engineering, takes the driver through a seemingly never-ending series of tunnels, around sharp bends and over bridges spanning gorges, to the constant accompaniment of convoys of trucks from all over Europe and beyond. Not my favourite stretch of road by a long chalk.

I sat back and took a closer look at her, and memories of the Hasani case came flooding back. I remembered now how impenetrable she had been under interrogation and how she had stonewalled every question even when it had become quite clear that she was only incriminating herself more by staying silent. I had told her at the time that by talking, she would probably have been able to avoid incarceration completely, but to no effect. She had stuck with stubborn silence to the bitter end and I had felt sorry for her at the time, although I had shared the judge's frustration. She had clearly been following somebody's orders when she had consistently refused to say more than the bare minimum. This might have been out of deep love or at least loyalty to Carnevale, or something more sinister. And when I say 'sinister', the first thing to come to mind is an organisation that not only demands but thrives upon secrecy and brutal violence.

This of course is what the Sicilians call Cosa Nostra.

Cosa Nostra or, in more general terms, the Mafia, covers a multitude of sins – quite literally. Just as music can consist of any number of different genres from opera to jazz and from madrigals to rap, so organised crime in Italy can mean anything from the Neapolitan Camorra to the Sicilian Mafia or the very nasty 'Ndrangheta of Calabria and any number of offshoots of these main branches, not to mention imported groups from as far away as China. So far in my investigative career over here in Tuscany, I hadn't come into direct contact with any of these and I had every intention of keeping it that way. Waking up to find a horse's head on the pillow beside me is not my idea of a fun way to earn my living. I decided to put her on the spot.

'Is there any possibility that the murder – if it was one – might be connected in some way with the criminal underworld? The Mafia, for want of another word?'

She shook her head decisively – but not completely convincingly. I remembered liking her in spite of everything. She had a university degree so she was clearly well educated and bright – unlike most gangsters' molls I had met – but she had evidently got herself into bad company. I felt pretty sure she knew more than she was saying but I knew from past experience that I was only going to hear what she wanted me to hear.

'I can't see why. My pop's a wealthy man and I'm sure he's

never been involved with that kind of thing and I certainly am not. As for the victim, why would the Mafia murder a Brit?'

'Can I ask how your father came by his money?' I still wasn't convinced.

'He lived and worked in the USA for thirty years and that's where he made it.'

'Doing what?'

'Restaurants. He had a chain of restaurants in New York City until he sold up a few years ago and came back to Italy.'

'I see. Is he American?'

'He is now. He's originally Italian; he moved to London when he was in his twenties, married another expat Italian and then our family emigrated to the States a year or two after I was born. He got US citizenship fifteen years ago.'

'But you didn't?'

'Like I say, I was born in London but we emigrated when I was only two. I lived in the US until I was twelve and then my mum and I came back to London.'

'But your dad stayed on in New York?'

She nodded.

'Did they divorce?'

'Afraid so.' Her voice was expressionless.

'I'm sorry. Divorces are tough on everybody, including the kids.'

'Don't I know it!'

I struggled to chase away memories of my own divorce. 'But you've stayed in contact with your father?'

'Yes, like I say, I've been staying with him for a couple of weeks now, taking a bit of a break. We get on really well now that he isn't working all hours in the restaurant.'

'Taking a break? Do you mind telling me what you're taking a break from? What do you do these days? Hopefully, you're out of the drug trade forever.'

She nodded vigorously. 'One thing's for certain, I'm not going back inside. No, I'm legit these days. I'm in the middle of a PhD in political science at King's and I'm having a holiday before diving back into my doctoral thesis on, don't laugh, *The Consequences of Chronic Overcrowding in the UK Penal System.*' She smiled. 'After all, I do have the sort of first-hand experience most students can only dream of...' her smile faded '...or have nightmares about.'

I was genuinely impressed. Assuming she was telling the truth, this was a remarkable success story. 'So you'd like me to go up to Liguria to see for myself?'

'Please, if you can spare the time.' She sounded genuinely pleading.

'Okay, but first let me ask you something else: why me? There are investigation agencies all over Italy. I imagine your dad speaks Italian like you do, so there was no need to choose an English-speaking PI. In fact, I can give you the name of a very good firm in Genoa if you like, which will be much closer to your dad's home.' I met her eye and repeated the question. 'Why me?'

'That's easy. It's because you're a good detective and, above all, you're straight. I know I can trust you. Not like some of your scumbag colleagues in the Met.' Before I could object to this sweeping indictment of the Metropolitan Police, she held up her hand. 'Not all of them, I know, but I've come across quite a few bent ones that I wouldn't trust as far as I could throw them. I've come to you because I know I can rely on you to do a good, thorough job.'

I was more than mildly surprised. Considering that I'd been responsible for depriving her of her freedom, she was sounding unexpectedly pragmatic – maybe a bit too pragmatic. The doubt circulating in my head ever since she had first started speaking refused to go away. Was this a set-up, an attempt to get back at me? Reluctantly, I let myself be persuaded into going to meet her father in two days' time and I took down his name and address. The name of the village, San Clemente, wasn't familiar but she told me it wasn't far from Alassio, which, by coincidence, was where Anna, my girlfriend, was taking me to celebrate my fifty-seventh birthday in just over two weeks' time – although I still wasn't sure whether a fifty-seventh birthday was something to be celebrated or lamented.

I already knew that the train would take me something like five hours or more with several changes, so I thought it best to drive up and stay the night in a local hotel rather than face the return journey the same day. Before I could tell her what I intended to do, she told me that her father had bags of room at his place and had insisted I stay with him. I thanked her but pointed at my canine companion.

'How would he feel about Oscar coming with me? I could leave him with my girlfriend if he prefers.'

'No problem at all. I'd already told him that you and Oscar come as a package deal and Pop says that's fine. I have to go away on Wednesday for a couple of nights, but I'll be back on Friday for two or three more weeks, so if you can stay two nights, I look forward to seeing you again.'

She then insisted on paying for two days of my time in full in advance – in crisp, new euro notes. Presumably, she wanted to be sure that I wouldn't change my mind.

2

TUESDAY EVENING

Anna drove up to my place at five o'clock and when she stepped out of the car, she was looking amazing, wearing a long, ruby-red gown modelled on the dress worn by a noblewoman in a painting by Bronzino. She smiled when she saw me in my outfit and she had the decency not to laugh, although I was under no illusions as to how I looked. I was wearing a bright yellow and red striped doublet, baggy pantaloons, and red tights that were far too tight around the nether regions. To complete the image, I also had a floppy hat on my head that hung down over one ear. As a look, it wasn't flattering. Even Oscar had been eyeing me strangely.

We were going to a medieval fair and Anna had insisted that we should dress accordingly. Our costumes were relics from the previous autumn when she and I had been involved with a Hollywood company making a movie, set in Renaissance Florence. Mine had been packed away on the top of the wardrobe ever since and as far as I was concerned that was where it should have stayed. Still, I knew that as she was a lecturer in medieval and Renaissance studies, this was Anna's thing, so the least I could do was to support her by dressing up – but preferably as rarely as possible.

The little town where the fair was taking place is only about ten kilometres beyond where I live in the hills just to the south-west of Florence. I loaded Oscar into the back of my battered old van rather than her car – one vehicle full of dog hair is enough – and we set off down the track towards the main road. Even though I drive down this bumpy track almost every day, I still haven't tired of the view. The track itself is flanked by statuesque cypress trees at regular intervals and it curls down the hill between olive groves and vineyards like a picture postcard. Ahead, the panorama extends out over the valley of the River Arno as far as the distant Apennines beyond. There was no doubt about it, my decision to settle in Tuscany two years ago was one of the best of my life and I could feel a smile forming on my face – in spite of the fact that my tights were killing me.

The smile was wiped from my face a few kilometres later when a yellow warning light on the dashboard came on to indicate that I was running low on fuel. There was a petrol station barely a kilometre ahead so that wasn't the problem. The problem was that I then found myself having to use a self-service pump in a busy roadside petrol station dressed like something out of a medieval tapestry. The driver filling up his white van alongside me shot me a grin.

'I thought you people used horses.'

I did my best to sound blasé. 'It would be cheaper to feed a horse than to feed this thing.'

The cost of the fuel was the least of my problems. When I went into the shop to pay, I suddenly remembered that my wallet was in the pocket of my tennis shorts underneath my velvet pantaloons and I had to shuffle off to a corner of the shop and rummage in my undergarments to retrieve my cash. I hoped nobody was planning on reviewing the CCTV footage and posting it on social media.

It was therefore with considerable relief when we finally arrived at the little village of San Giorgio Alto and I found that many of the other people climbing out of cars for the medieval fair were also dressed up in a similar manner to us. As a result, I began to relax and I even approved when Anna produced a rather fine plaited red and yellow ribbon that she used to fashion a stylish medieval lead for Oscar. I just hoped he wouldn't try and eat it – he eats most things.

We walked in through the arched gateway in the dilapidated, medieval walls and along a narrow, stone-paved street flanked by stalls selling plastic swords and shields, commemorative T-shirts and all sorts of foods ranging from candyfloss to a whole pig roasting on a spit. Needless to say, Oscar's medieval lead earned its keep as I discouraged my ever-hungry dog from investigating the food stalls too closely.

Less than a hundred yards further on, the street opened into a small piazza with a fine old Romanesque church directly in front of us. Straw bales had been set up so as to form a ring in the centre of the square, where a man and a woman dressed in full medieval costume were demonstrating the ancient art of falconry. Anna and I watched for a while and then strolled around. When we came to the church, I waited outside with Oscar while she went in to check it out.

There was still a lot of heat in the sun even though it was almost six o'clock and I, like many of the spectators, hugged what shade there was. Coincidentally – or so I told Anna afterwards – this happened to be right beside a stall selling wine and, as I thought it only right to support local commerce, I bought two paper cups of cold rosé. When Anna emerged from the church, we sat on the end of an ancient stone bench and sipped our wine.

I had already told her about my having to go north next morning and she expressed regret that she couldn't come with me but, of course, she had to work. Even though the end of term was now in sight, she still had a lot of bureaucracy to sort out, papers to mark and preparations to make for the autumn term. I gave her an encouraging smile.

'Don't worry, you and I'll be on the Riviera together in two weeks' time.'

She leant over and gave me a little kiss on the cheek. 'It'll be good to get away together, just us two.' Oscar looked up from where he was sprawled on the ground at our feet and she hastily qualified what she had just said. 'When I say us two, I of course mean us three. Do you think tomorrow's trip is going to be a waste of time for you or might there be something else behind this woman's story? It strikes me as unusual, to say the least, that somebody you were responsible for putting in jail should come to you for help. Just you be careful. I wouldn't want this to be some kind of hoax or, even worse, like an attempt to incriminate you in return or even kill you.'

I nodded. 'The same thought had occurred to me, but I can't really see how something like that could be arranged. The police up there can hardly accuse me of murder considering that I was down here in Florence, three hundred kilometres away, when the alleged murder took place. And if the bad guys – whoever they are – are luring me away to murder me, I don't see why they need to go to all that trouble.' I could see the concern on her face so I produced a little smile. 'All they need to do is push me off the Ponte Vecchio. A few mouthfuls of River Arno water would probably kill me most effectively. Have you seen what colour it is these days?'

'Well, just be careful.' She gave me another kiss. 'I wouldn't want anything to happen to you.'

I kissed her back. 'And neither would I. Don't worry, I've got Oscar to protect me.'

He opened one eye at the sound of his name but made no attempt to rouse himself from his comatose state. When evolution was handing out guard-dog genes, it only really gave most Labradors the bare minimum, compensating by overloading them with the gluttony gene. Still, I couldn't complain. My canine best buddy had demonstrated his worth on numerous occasions. He maybe wasn't quite on the same level as my old sergeant, now Inspector Paul Wilson, at the Metropolitan Police, when it came to police procedure, but he made up for it with unswerving loyalty and he had baled me out of a number of dodgy situations already.

As the sun gradually sank lower towards the horizon, we walked around the little town and climbed the steps onto the top of the city wall. I'm sure that Health and Safety back in the UK wouldn't have approved of the fact that there was absolutely no barrier on the inside of the battlements and a drop of about thirty feet to the ground. On the outside, the drop was enhanced by the fact that the ground sloped steeply downwards and I drew back apprehensively. I've never been very good with heights and so, after a quick look at the view and a couple of photos, I wasted no time in following Oscar back down again, carefully shepherding Anna, who was struggling with her heavy velvet skirt that completely hid her feet.

Instead of a sit-down meal that evening, we opted for some Tuscan fast food. This consisted of a couple of focaccia sandwiches made with *porchetta*. The lady behind the counter filled the sandwiches with hand-carved slices of the tender, deboned pork from a roasted roll of meat, glazed a wonderful chestnut brown on the outside. The texture was soft and the taste was enhanced by the addition of rosemary and, in particular, fennel, which gave it its distinctive flavour. We accompanied this with cups of Chianti and consumed our meal perched on a straw bale as we watched knights in full armour beating the hell out of each other in the ring. Although I was sure the sheet steel they were wearing was strong enough to avoid blood being drawn, I had little doubt that most of the performers would wake up next morning covered in bruises. When it comes to medieval authenticity, the Tuscans take it very seriously. I reflected that, in comparison, having to wander around in red tights was far less of a sacrifice – however uncomfortable they might be.

The warring knights were followed by a colourful display of flag swirling, a trio of jugglers, and then a troop of traditional dancers, accompanied by a little band playing authentic-looking, medieval instruments. All in all, it was an interesting, fun and atmospheric evening and we were both in good spirits when we finally headed back to the van just after eleven. It was as we took our seats inside the van that Anna dropped her bombshell.

She turned towards me and laid her hand on my thigh. I could see her eyes sparkling in the orange glow of a distant streetlight. 'We do get on so very well together, don't we, Dan? We're spending more and more time together these days. I was wondering, do you think it would make sense for us to move in together?'

Looking back on it, I now know that my response should have been an immediate and unequivocal yes. Instead, idiot that I am, all I could manage to say was, 'Umm...'

'Umm? Could you translate, please?' She removed her hand from my leg and sat up straight, staring forwards out of the windscreen.

There was an edge to her voice and I was gradually beginning to realise the extent to which I had put my foot in it. The fact was, however, that I'd been divorced now for less than two years and, after the abject failure of that relationship, there was something deep down inside me that was urging caution. I took a deep breath and did my best to explain.

'I'd love that, Anna. You're right, we do spend most of our free time together and we get on so very well.' I risked a glance across at the side of her face but could read nothing in her expression. 'It's just that...'

Anna's a very bright woman and after seven months together, she knew me well. 'You aren't ready for a long-term commitment.' Her tone wasn't unkind, but I didn't need to be a detective to hear the undercurrent of hurt in it. I hastened to elaborate, hoping desperately that I wasn't digging myself deeper into this particular hole.

'No... yes, I don't know. Everything's been going so well between us; I'm terrified of jinxing it. What if we start living together and you discover things about me that put you off?'

I managed to stop myself in time before suggesting that I might discover things about *her* that *I* didn't like, but the damage had been done. I stopped talking and waited for her to respond, but I waited in vain. She didn't argue, she didn't object, she didn't attempt to reason with me. She clammed up and didn't say a word all the way home, in spite of a few hesitant attempts by me to engage her in some sort of conversation. My assumption had been that she would stay at my place that night, but when we got back to my house and climbed out of the van, she headed straight for her own car. By the time I had gone round to the back of the van and let Oscar out, she was already in the driving seat.

I went over to say something, anything, but she just gave me a dismissive wave of the hand and set off down the track. As I stood there helplessly, I felt a nose prod my leg. I glanced down to see my dog looking at me with an expression on his face that needed no words. I knew I was an idiot, and he knew I was an idiot, and he knew there was no point reminding me.

3

WEDNESDAY LUNCHTIME

The drive up north on Wednesday morning was as wearing as I had expected and I was feeling pretty frazzled by the time I reached my destination. In spite of the aircon, I was hot and sweaty even though I'd stopped for a quick break at Chiavari, where both Oscar and I had gone into the sea for a swim. This, followed by an excellent peach and white chocolate ice cream for me and one of his big dog biscuits and a bowl of cool water for him, had been very refreshing at the time, but now I could feel salt crusting on my skin and I was dying for a shower. The lingering aroma of damp Labrador in my ageing VW van didn't do anything to improve the atmosphere either. Or my mood.

I hadn't slept well the previous night after my final exchange with Anna. At six o'clock in the morning, I had got out of bed and seriously considered calling her, but in the end had chickened out and sent her a brief text.

I'm so sorry. How could I be so stupid? You just took me by surprise. Of course I want a long-term relationship with you. I love you dearly

and you need to know that I'll do whatever it takes to make you
happy. x

As I drove in and out of the interminable succession of
tunnels on the busy motorway, I turned over and over in my head
what she'd said to me and what I'd said to her and, in particular,
what I hadn't said to her, but should have done. I was under no
illusion that Anna had brought joy and love into my life at a time
when I had been feeling emotionally shattered after the divorce.
The idea of losing her was as awful as the idea of losing Oscar.
For a moment, I questioned whether even this assertion could
have been misinterpreted if I had said it to her. Oscar is my best
buddy and he's been with me through thick and thin but, surely,
the love between a man and a woman should exceed the love of a
man for a dumb animal. This, however, was definitely one can of
worms that I wasn't going to open, so I did my best to relegate my
tattered personal life and concentrate on what lay before me on
the Riviera.

In spite of Anna's doubts and my misgivings about the true
motivation behind Bianca Moretti's appeal for help, business was
business and my natural curiosity meant that I was looking
forward to meeting her father and finding out what had really
happened last Saturday night – if, indeed, he was a real relative of
hers and not just some random acquaintance. I only had her
word for it that they were related and I was taking anything she
said with a liberal pinch of salt.

After the usual traffic chaos around Genoa and some stop-
start crawling through a series of tunnels – some brightly illuminated and others virtually pitch dark – the road turned west
towards France and the traffic speeded up again. The autostrada
ran parallel to the Riviera coast and there were beautiful views
out across the intense blue of the Mediterranean, where no doubt

the seaside resorts were bracing themselves for the main holiday season that would start in just over two weeks when the schools broke up for the summer. I felt sure that at that point, the traffic along here would get even worse and I was glad my birthday celebrations up here would be just before the great getaway.

Not long after seeing a sign announcing that the French border was sixty-five kilometres ahead, I reached my turn-off, went through the automatic pay toll and followed the signs inland up a broad valley for three kilometres as instructed. On either side of me were polytunnels, greenhouses and fields filled with everything from soft fruit to aubergines. Roadside shops and stalls advertised all manner of locally grown fruit and veg as well as wine and olive oil. I made a mental note to stock up before heading back south again. As I approached the village of San Clemente, I caught sight of a blue and white sign marked *La Torre Retreat* – the last word in English – indicating that this was five hundred metres ahead. *Torre* in Italian means tower, and high above me to the left I could see the unmistakable shape of a tower, standing out against the light-blue sky. I turned off at another blue and white arrow just before the church and started to climb seriously.

The increasingly narrow road wound its way up the hillside initially between modern villas, no doubt many of them holiday homes owned by people from the big industrial cities like Turin and Milan, before the houses gradually gave way to olive groves and vineyards that were then replaced by straggly clumps of bamboo and oleander and then little more than barren scrub and occasional hardy pine trees on the steeply sloping hillside. As I approached the hilltop, the tarmac deteriorated into a gravel track and I bumped up the last hundred metres or so, taking care to avoid any potholes. I heard movement behind me and saw Oscar's face appear above the back seat. He looked as pleased to be nearing the end of the drive as I was.

'It's all right, dog, we're here.'

His tail started to wag as I turned the last corner and found myself confronted by a sign pointing straight on towards a wooden chalet and what looked like a checkpoint with a red and white barrier across the road. The sign announced this as *La Torre Retreat*. However, as instructed by Bianca Moretti, I stopped fifty metres short of it at a sturdy pair of gates set into solid gateposts with a wire fence stretching off on either side. On the left gatepost was a bell push and an intercom. I got out to ring the bell and the heat hit me like a physical slap. Clearly the heatwave extended as far north as here. Before I could reach out and press the button, a metallic voice emanated from the grill.

'Mr Armstrong, I presume.'

For a moment, I had a flashback to one of the James Bond movies where the evil genius greets the arrival of 007 with almost the same words, and for a moment I wondered whether the owner of the voice at the other end of this communication device was currently stroking a Persian cat. He was speaking fluent English and his accent was unmistakably American and, although I'm not too good at distinguishing the different parts of the US, I had seen enough episodes of *NYPD Blue* to know a New York accent when I heard one.

'Yes, it's me. Can I drive in or do I leave the car here?'

'Bring it in.'

A yellow light on the gatepost started flashing and I heard an electrical whine as the gates began to open so I got back into the van and drove on through. The track continued for another fifty yards or so until I reached the base of the tower where there was a gravelled parking area. This contained a Toyota pickup truck and a lone umbrella pine, which, while a big tree, was dwarfed by the tower behind it. Seen close up, the stone tower was square and quite a lot bigger than I had first thought, and I counted windows on four floors before the crenelations on the top. It looked very old – Anna would have known better, but to me it looked medieval – and it was clearly very, very solid. It was also very beautiful and the commanding views down the valley to the sea were delightful from here at the base, and no doubt outstanding from the top. However, my pleasure at the view was immediately eclipsed as thoughts of Anna returned my mind to the mess I had made of things the previous night. If only she would call me or reply to my text.

Struggling unsuccessfully to dismiss this depressing subject and concentrate on the here and now, I parked in the shade of the tree and climbed out, stretching as I did so. Oscar surveyed me from inside with a hopeful expression on his face and I was just wondering whether it would be all right for me to let him out when my attention was attracted by a noise from the massive, old, wooden door set in the base of the tower. The door opened with a hint of a creak and I found myself confronted by Bianca Moretti's father – assuming he was who she had said he was – Leonardo Moretti.

From where I was standing, I could see that he probably barely came up to my shoulder but he made up for his lack of height by his width. He had shoulders like a bull and hands like hams. He was carrying quite a few excess pounds around his waist but he was still a powerful-looking man. He looked friendly enough and I went over to the base of the stone steps to greet him.

'Mr Moretti? I'm pleased to meet you.' I turned and pointed back to the van, where Oscar's black face was pressed up against the glass. 'And that's Oscar in the van. Bianca said you wouldn't mind if I brought him. Are you sure?'

'Does he bite?' Close up, I could see a distinct resemblance to Bianca so that added credence to her description of him as her father. I sought to reassure him as far as my dog was concerned.

'He only bites food.'

His expression lightened. 'Food, I got. Bring him in.' I rather got the impression that Leonardo Moretti was a man of few words.

I went back and opened the boot. Oscar jumped out happily and, after liberally irrigating the umbrella pine, trotted up the steps to say hello to Mr Moretti, and the man's expression definitely softened as he bent down to stroke Oscar's head.

'Good-looking dog. I like dogs.' As I came up the steps again, he transferred his attention back to me. 'You eaten? Like I say, I got food.' He smiled. 'Not just dog food.'

'I had an ice cream a few hours ago but otherwise, no, I haven't eaten.'

'Me neither. Come on in.' He held out one of his massive hands towards me and I shook it, bracing myself for a crushing handshake, but was relieved to find that he was remarkably gentle.

Oscar and I followed him into a fairly barren entrance hall and on up the stairs. This was a gently curving stone staircase that led up to the first floor, where I found myself in an unexpectedly charming room. Given the fortress-like exterior and the utilitarian air of the entranceway and stone steps, I had been expecting bare, medieval austerity designed for a garrison of soldiers, but, instead, this large room could have come straight out of a twenty-first-century interior design magazine. The old, terracotta floor tiles had been liberally scattered with what looked to my untrained eye like expensive Persian carpets and two huge, white, leather sofas were positioned in front of the old, stone fireplace. Over to one side of the room was a magnificent kitchen area, where I counted no fewer than four ovens. Of course, if my host had been in the restaurant trade, he probably wanted to keep his hand in. This of course did bode well for me getting a fine lunch and I realised I was hungry. As for Oscar, he's always hungry.

'Drink?'

I nodded. 'Thanks, whatever you're having, and could Oscar have a bowl of water, do you think?'

He gave no reply but headed to a fridge the size of a walk-in wardrobe and reappeared with two cans of Budweiser. He then filled a bowl with water and put it on the floor for Oscar, who lapped it up gratefully, splashing water all over the place as he did so. I apologised for the mess but Moretti just waved away my apologies, handed me a can of beer, opened his and held it up towards me in greeting.

'Good of you to come. Thanks.'

By this time, I could see where Bianca Moretti got her taciturn nature from. It presumably ran in the family. I took a very welcome mouthful of cold beer and watched as Moretti set about preparing lunch.

'You like pasta.'

The way he said it indicated that he couldn't imagine anybody who didn't like the stuff. Fortunately, I do and I was able to reassure him. Then, in the space of barely a minute, he had put a pan of water on the stove to boil and had brought a packet of smoked pancetta and three eggs from the fridge.

'Carbonara okay?'

I've always liked *pasta alla carbonara* and often prepare it myself. It's quick, easy and tasty, particularly when the eggs are really fresh. While waiting for the water to boil, he produced a leg of cured ham from a wall cupboard and pulled a vicious-looking knife from a drawer.

'Ham and melon?'

Without waiting for my answer, he started carving the ham. This was supported on a solid iron frame and I saw at once that I was in the presence of an expert. The joint of ham was already about halfway through and with deceptive ease, he cut away a paper-thin slice of the meat from the exposed area and glanced across at me.

'Okay to give it to the dog?'

I'm convinced I saw Oscar nod his head. When it comes to food, Labradors have remarkable comprehension skills. I also nodded and Moretti handed down the slice of meat and Oscar took it from him with considerable restraint and respect before swallowing it whole.

Moretti waved towards a door in the wall. 'Wanna wash up?'

By the time I returned from the top-of-the-range, modern bathroom, I found that he had already divided the beautiful, orange-fleshed melon into slices and these, along with a plate of freshly carved ham, were sitting on a fine old oak table over on the far side of the room.

'Take a seat.'

I did as instructed and seconds later, there were glasses and bottles of mineral water and red wine in front of me. The glasses were workmanlike tumblers rather than long-stemmed wine glasses, and that was fine with me. He handed me a corkscrew and indicated that I should open the bottle. It was a three-year-old Nebbiolo, a close relative of its better-known cousin, Barolo, and one of my favourite Piedmontese wines. While I was studying the label, Moretti came back with a round loaf of crusty bread the size of a bowler hat, and a bread knife.

'Freshly baked this morning.'

I gave him an appreciative look. 'You do your own baking?'

'It gives me something to do. I don't get out much.'

'What about the campsite, the Retreat?'

'I got guys to do that. Besides, I don't have the body for it any longer.'

I was still trying to work out what he could mean by that when he pointed at the ham and melon.

'Let's eat. We can talk after.'

The meal was flawless in its simplicity. The melon was succulent and ripe, the ham excellent with just a hint of saltiness, and the pasta perfectly cooked. I watched in open admiration as he seemed to know exactly when the pasta was ready even from a distance and without, as far as I had noticed, looking at his watch. He went across to the hob, picked the pan off the gas and took it over to the sink. There he poured out most, but not all, of the water from the pan, brought it over to the table and threw in three egg yolks, the chopped pancetta that had been simmering on a low heat and a single clove of garlic. He turned the mixture over expertly with two spoons while the egg instantly cooked in the heat. Finally, he added pepper from a grinder almost the size of a baseball bat and then served up three portions: one for me, one for him and one for Oscar. A little smile appeared on his face.

'Only fair the dog gets good food. Better let his cool first.'

The pasta was excellent and although he'd given me a massive portion, I finished it willingly. By that time, the pasta on Oscar's plate had cooled sufficiently and this was handed down to him for his opinion. As always, he hoovered it up in next to no time and licked the bowl sparkling clean, pushing it around the room with his nose as he did so. He then spent another happy five minutes licking his lips, which was probably about as close as Moretti was going to get to an accolade for his cooking from my dog.

At last, over a bowl of fresh cherries, I brought up the reason why I'd come. 'I gather there's been a death at the camp. Bianca says you both think it was murder. Want to tell me all about it?'

He took a big mouthful of the extremely good wine before speaking. 'It's not what you think.'

I waited for more but none was forthcoming so I tried a little bit of prodding. 'And what do I think?'

He gave me a searching look. 'Italo-American, made a pile in New York, living in a castle in Italy – it's gotta be I'm hiding either from the police or the mob. Be straight with me, isn't that what you came here thinking?'

I owed him the truth so I nodded. 'Let's just say it was a thought I had – along with a lot of others. I don't like to prejudge people without having all the facts, but you probably know the background to how Bianca and I know each other. I had no idea what sort of person you would turn out to be.' Before he could take offence, I hastened to add, 'And from what I've seen so far, you're one of the good guys.'

He shook his head ruefully. 'Thanks for that. Bianca's a good girl too, deep down. She got into bad company over there in England and she paid the price.' He caught my eye. 'She told me you're the guy who put her in jail.'

I nodded again. 'Afraid so, but she didn't do herself any favours. For some reason, she wouldn't cooperate, she wouldn't say a word and, in the end, the judge had no option. I have to admit, I had a feeling that because of her Italian background, she might have been involved with organised crime – and you know what that means.'

'I sure do. I've met my share of mobsters over the years. Hell, I've fed some of the most infamous mafiosi in New York. But that doesn't mean I'm one of them and it doesn't make her one of them either.'

'So why didn't she cooperate? Why didn't she speak out to help herself?'

He shrugged. 'Why do women do anything? Only she can tell you. Me, I reckon it was love, or infatuation at least. She always had a habit of hooking up with bums.'

'Anyway, returning to the death of the man on Saturday, what was his name?'

'Joseph Beck. He called himself Joe.'

'I'd like to hear everything you can tell me about him.'

4

WEDNESDAY AFTERNOON

Leonardo Moretti sat back in his chair and tapped his fingers together as he reflected.

'I got to know the guy. Well, sort of. I'm sixty-seven and he was at least twenty years younger than me, say mid-forties, but we got on okay. He was in good shape, kept himself fit, he swam a lot and hit the gym every day he was here. This was his second time here. He came for two weeks last July and I first struck up a friendship with him then. We talked over the fence most days. I used to see him jogging around the perimeter every morning and evening. This year, he'd been here for almost two weeks before his death and he'd booked to stay for a whole month. He was staying in one of our chalets.'

'And what did you and Mr Beck talk about, Mr Moretti?'

'Leo, call me Leo.'

'Thanks, and I'm Dan. So, did he tell you anything interesting?'

'That's what I've been trying to remember. He didn't talk about himself apart from saying he came from London. I asked him if he worked and he said yes, but he said it in a way that clearly indicated he didn't want to talk about it. I've been dealing with customers all my life so I didn't press him. That was his own affair, not mine.'

'Would you say he was unduly reticent?'

He paused for thought. 'It was pretty clear he didn't want to talk about his work but, like I say, what the hell?'

'Was there anything particularly memorable about him?'

This time, Leo nodded immediately. 'A couple of things, starting with the fact that he spoke excellent Italian and totally fluent-sounding German. I don't speak German but the guys at the Retreat said he sounded like the real McCoy. I certainly heard him chatting to some of our Italian guests and he sounded very convincing. When he and I talked, it was in English and he was as fluent as we are – with a posher English accent than yours.'

'There's nothing posh about me. Did he tell you how come he spoke so fluently?'

'For my money, he must have spent quite some time in Italy and in Germany. That's the only way to get so good at a language. Bianca speaks fluent English and Italian, so maybe he learned from his parents like she did, but, however he did it, he was good.' He added an aside. 'My ex-wife's Italian so we always spoke it together in the house.'

'You mentioned a *couple* of things. What else struck you apart from his fluency in the three languages?'

'It looked very much to me as if he had a bullet wound in his stomach.' Seeing my expression of surprise, he specified, 'Not a fresh one, just a scar, all healed up.'

'You don't think it could have been an operation scar?'

'If it was, the surgeon did a terrible job. It was a jagged scar, three or four inches below his navel, and it looked like something white had gone splat on his stomach.'

'How come you could see his lower abdomen?'

He looked surprised for a moment and then stood up. 'Feel like climbing some stairs?'

I nodded and followed him up three more flights of stairs that led up through the second and third floors and finally out onto the flat roof of the tower. The view from up here was fantastic. The heat haze made things a bit indistinct but I could still see for miles and miles along the coast in either direction. I could see a huge cruise ship heading west from Genoa, probably bound for Monte Carlo or somewhere along the Côte d'Azur, and a flotilla of tiny yachts with bright-red sails near the harbour of San Clemente Spiaggia, the nearby beach. Looking inland, there were rows of deep-green, tree-covered hills with occasional clusters of red-roofed villages dotted around. But it immediately became clear that Leo hadn't brought me up here to admire the panorama. He pointed down to the campsite below us, just along the ridge from the tower.

There were probably a dozen tents, predominantly white, orange and blue in colour, along with a similar number of mostly white caravans and camper vans. Behind them were four rows of wooden chalets, with three larger ones at one end. There were various low, whitewashed buildings, presumably bath houses and toilets, a bigger building with tables and parasols outside, where I could see people eating and drinking. A large swimming pool in the middle of the complex added to the holiday look of the place. People were splashing about in the water or lying on the array of sunbeds that surrounded the pool. As I looked on, I suddenly realised why Leo had brought me up here and how he had managed to get such a good view of the victim's presumed bullet wound.

Every single person down below me in *La Torre Retreat* was stark naked.

I turned back towards him. 'It's a nudist camp?'

He tut-tutted. 'We prefer naturist. This is a naturist retreat where like-minded people can strip off and live their lives as nature intended.'

'I see. And what do you think the attraction of the place was for Mr Beck?'

Leo gave me a little smile. 'He even cracked a joke about that. He said, "At least this way, there's no chance of anybody carrying a concealed weapon." I wondered at the time what made him say that. Just for fun or...? Who knows?'

I stood there and surveyed the view for quite some time, idly reflecting that, from what I could see from up here, the majority of visitors to the Retreat appeared to be considerably older than I was. I also couldn't help noticing that very few of them would have stood a chance in a beauty contest, but that clearly didn't bother them one bit, so more power to their suntanned elbows and, indeed, the rest of the considerable expanses of skin on display. I thought about what Leo had just told me and I had to admit that I was feeling curious to know more about the mysterious Joseph Beck. Who had he been: a harmless, trilingual Brit with a penchant for letting it all hang out or somebody altogether less clear-cut?

One thing was for sure: I knew I would have loved to get my hands on the police report. Had his death really been a simple accident or might there have been a more sinister reason behind it? Unfortunately, the days of DCI Armstrong had ended two years earlier so I knew there was no point even trying to get sight of the report. That was a police affair and I was no longer in the police. But maybe if I took a look around, I might discover something of interest, although, four days on from his death, I imagined any clues would have long since disappeared.

No sooner did I think about looking around the camp than an unsettling thought occurred to me.

'Leo, if I want to take a look around the Retreat, sniff about and maybe talk to a few people, can I go in dressed like this or do I have to strip off and join in with the fun?'

'It depends what you want to be seen as. Obviously, tradesmen and emergency services are allowed in wearing normal clothes, but anybody fully dressed is immediately recognised as an outsider, so if you were thinking of trying to question people without arousing suspicion, I'm afraid you don't have much choice.' I saw his eyes survey me for a moment. 'You look like you keep yourself in good shape. You'll be fine.'

I felt a nose nudge my knee and I looked down to see Oscar with an expression on his face that was difficult to read. Not wanting to give him more credit than he was due, I assumed he was just trying to tell me he felt it was time for a comfort break, but there was a distinct glint in his eyes all the same. Did the expression on his face indicate that he knew about the spare tyre and 'love handles' gradually developing at my waist in spite of my best efforts to shed them? He knew and I knew that, of the two of us, Oscar definitely looks better unclothed then I do. Still, I told myself, new experiences make life interesting, but I had to admit to feeling more than a little apprehensive at the thought of wandering around in the altogether.

Before taking the plunge and heading to the naturist camp, I decided I'd better find out everything Leo knew about the dead man. 'Did the police say when Beck died?'

'I heard that the pathologist wasn't completely sure but he reckoned he'd been in the water for about six to eight hours.'

'And what time on Sunday morning was he found?'

'Just after six, so they said that meant he must have died some time just before midnight.'

'Would there have been many people still up and about at that time of night?'

He shook his head. 'Not last Saturday. Some weeks, we have entertainment in the clubhouse, a dance band or a singer, but last Saturday there was nothing. It's only really the start of the season for us and there's a lot more on offer when high summer comes. The clubhouse closes at midnight and by that time, Freddie said there was hardly anybody left there.'

'Freddie. Who's he?'

'She, not he. Federica's our catering manager. Everybody calls her Freddie.'

'What about Beck? You said the police reckoned he'd been drinking heavily; was that at the clubhouse bar?'

He shook his head again. 'No, the police asked that as well, but although he ate there around eight on Saturday night, he then disappeared off to his chalet around nine-thirty. He had a habit of going for a late-night swim most nights before turning in and the police say they found an almost empty bottle of Scotch in the bushes by the pool with his prints on it. They reckon he must have gone down there at midnight, drunk himself into a stupor for whatever reason and then decided to go for a swim. They said he was so hammered, he must have slipped and knocked himself out before falling in and drowning. There were bloodstains on the stone edge of the pool where he hit himself.'

'And he was here on his own? He didn't have a partner or friend with him?' I saw Leo shake his head and I moved on to the next logical question. 'What about other people here at the camp... sorry, the Retreat? Did he make friends? Was he particularly close to anybody? Was there somebody who might have joined him down at the pool for a drink or anything else? A woman maybe?'

'Nobody special as far as I know, but Freddie and the other staff would know better. Like I say, I don't go down there that much these days.' He glanced ruefully at his ample waistline. 'I

know I shouldn't be self-conscious but I am. Joe Beck was a
friendly enough guy but, even with me, he rarely stopped to talk
for more than a minute or two. He was a bit of a loner but, like I
say, what the hell? We're all different, aren't we?'

So why would someone want to murder this 'friendly enough
guy'? Unless there was a totally unhinged killer at the camp,
murdering at random, there had to be a reason. Did Joseph Beck
have a dark secret? Was he known to somebody else here? Who
had he been? What might he have done to warrant ending up
face down in a swimming pool? I moved on to practical questions.

'Who's in charge at the Retreat? Are you still hands-on or do
you have a manager?'

'I keep an eye on the finances mostly. George is the manager.
His full name is Giorgio Albenga, but everybody calls him
George. He's a local guy who spent time in the UK managing
hotels on the south coast of England before coming back to San
Clemente with his English wife. He speaks three or four
languages and he does a great job.'

'And what about documents? Do you keep guests' passports
or copy them?' In Italy, hoteliers are required by law to keep a
record of everybody staying in their establishments.

'We scan them into the computer. I'll ask George to send them
through to you if you want.'

'Yes please, and while you're at it, could you send me details of
all staff members including grounds staff, cleaners, everybody?' I
gave him one of my cards with my email as well as my mobile
number on it. 'Presumably, the police searched Beck's chalet; did
they find anything interesting or suspicious?'

'Apparently not, but I don't know how thoroughly they
searched. According to what one of the officers said to Freddie,
there was no reason to think it had been anything other than an
unfortunate accident.' He caught my eye. 'This came as a relief to

me because I'd been wondering if we might find ourselves in trouble with our insurers. As far as the police are concerned, he simply drank too much, fell and banged his head, slipped into the pool and drowned. There was nothing we could have done to stop him and in consequence, we bear no responsibility.'

'I have to ask: in that case, why am *I* here? Why are you and your daughter so keen to prove that the guy was murdered?'

'I liked the guy, what can I say? Bianca told me she knew a good PI and I thought, what the hell, why not? Let's say I hope you can satisfy my curiosity one way or another.'

This was a very altruistic attitude and my cynical side couldn't help questioning if there might be another reason why he wasn't just letting sleeping dogs lie, but for now I put that on the back burner. 'What about Bianca? Was she keen on the naturist life-style as well?'

He nodded. 'Very much so; in fact, she was the person who suggested I open a naturist retreat.'

'And what did she do here? She said she'd been with you for a couple of weeks; was that staying here in the tower or down at the Retreat?'

'When she comes over, she stays here with me. She has her own room upstairs and we mostly eat together, but she spends most of her days at the Retreat.'

'So did she know the victim?'

I felt pretty sure I spotted a fractional hesitation from him before he answered, but I didn't comment. 'She said she knew him by sight, but she didn't know him well.'

I took his word for it – for now – but it seemed to me that Leo wasn't telling me the whole truth. 'Apart from Joseph Beck being a bit of a loner, do you have any idea why he might have been killed and who might have done it?'

'No idea. He was a bit reticent but I never thought him suspicious, and all the staff liked him. As far as I'm aware, he didn't have any arguments or disagreements with anybody else. George and I have spoken to all the staff and none of us can think of anybody who might have had it in for him.'

I tried again. 'And what about Bianca – are you sure she didn't know him well?'

Once again, I was sure I spotted something in his eyes but it passed in a flash. 'Try asking her. She's gone off in my car for a couple of days but she'll be back on Friday.'

What, I wondered, had caused that momentary look of wariness? Was there a subplot here to which I wasn't being allowed access? Did they know more than they were telling me and, if so, why was that? For now, I carried on trying to establish the facts of what had happened. 'Could the killer have got in from outside?'

He shook his head decisively. 'No way. As you can probably imagine, a place like this attracts all sorts of weirdos and Peeping Toms. There's a seven-foot wire fence all the way round and a locked gate for people to go in and out. There are CCTV cameras on poles all around the perimeter as well. The police checked all the footage and it's quite clear that nobody got in that night.'

'What about CCTV inside the complex?'

He shook his head. 'None. For obvious reasons. The Retreat is a very discreet environment and we promise our guests complete privacy.'

'So if nobody could have got in, this almost certainly means that, if Beck was murdered, his killer must have been somebody already here at the Retreat.' Leo nodded grimly and I asked the hundred-thousand-dollar question. 'Are you sure you can't think of anybody here who might have done it?'

'Ever since Sunday morning, that's just about all I've been thinking about. Saturday's our changeover day and there were fifty-eight guests here that night plus Beck, roughly half of them fresh arrivals that day. It must have been one of them, but nobody stands out.'

'Could it have been a staff member?' Before he could object, I carried on. 'In a murder investigation, we always have to consider all options, however unlikely. Is there anybody on your staff that you think capable of doing something like that?'

'Nobody, hand on heart, I'm sure of that. Besides, for a murder, you need a motive, don't you? I reckon none of us here knew him more than casually.'

Or did they? The fact that Leo and his daughter were paying me to look into the death of a 'casual acquaintance' made me think that there had to be more to it than met the eye. Leo was a nice guy, but I felt sure he wasn't giving me the full story about this mysterious lone traveller. Deep down, I was convinced that Leo and Bianca had known Joseph Beck better than they were saying and, if so, why keep this a secret? What was there in Beck's past that couldn't be mentioned? For now, I decided against pressing Leo harder. There would be a time for that if I did discover that it hadn't been just a tragic accident.

'Tell me about the other guests. Are there many Brits here? If Beck was British and he really was murdered, then it's logical to wonder whether there might be a British connection.'

'I have the full list on the laptop downstairs – and, like I say, I'll see that you get a copy – but I know that there are only seven British passport holders: two couples, a pair of women in one of the luxury chalets and a single guy called Griffiths.'

'And are they still here now? In fact, has anybody left since the death of Mr Beck?'

'Only one couple. Mr and Mrs Schiffer from Munich left yesterday because their granddaughter was rushed to hospital. They're both in their eighties so I think it's unlikely they could have been involved in Beck's death. Otherwise, the people here now are the people who were here on Saturday night.'

This, at least, was promising. Fifty-eight people minus the two elderly Germans meant that there were now fifty-six possible suspects plus, whatever Leo might say, a question mark over the handful of staff members and his daughter if she'd been there at the time. Fifty-six was a big number and I could well understand why the investigating officer would have heaved a sigh of relief when the pathologist had come up with the information that there were no suspicious circumstances surrounding the death of Joseph Beck.

The question I now had was whether *I* was going to have to interview all fifty-six and, on a more practical note, how I was going to carry my notebook, pencil and phone if I was wandering around stark naked.

5

WEDNESDAY AFTERNOON

Just after three, Oscar and I walked along to the Retreat. Before leaving, Leo had given me a printout of the names of the current guests and where they were located around the site. After that, he showed me to my room on the second floor of the tower. This was stunning, with a sunken bath in the en suite bathroom like something out of *Cleopatra*. The views from the windows were incredible and I felt sure Anna would have been on cloud nine if she'd been with me. With her historical background, this would have been right up her street. Needless to say, thoughts of her revived memories of the previous night and I checked my phone yet again to see if there was any reply to my text. Once again, there was nothing. I must have given a sigh because Oscar wandered over and nudged me with his nose, no doubt sensing that I wasn't my usual reasonably happy self. I scratched his ears and realised, not for the first time, that he's much better at this emotional stuff than I am.

Repressing the urge to try calling Anna for fear of being accused of badgering her, I decided to concentrate on the job in hand and went downstairs to the first floor, where I found Leo doing the washing up. I offered to help but he thanked me and waved me away. He gave me a key to the main door and the gate and told me to come and go as I pleased. I was genuinely grateful. If he was a mafioso, he was hiding it well, although I still wasn't convinced that his simple explanation for why he'd engaged my services was as simple as all that. Still, that could wait. First, I had to check out the scene of the crime – although I had yet to hear any convincing reason why it might not just have been an unfortunate accident as the local police believed.

When I arrived at the Retreat, I wasn't sure quite what to expect. The first thing I saw was a graphic on the gate of a packet of cigarettes and a camera with red crosses through them. Clearly, these were forbidden on site. I was met by a man probably in his early thirties, dressed in shorts and a polo shirt with *La Torre Retreat* and a tower logo embroidered on his left breast above his name: Dario. He emerged from the gatekeeper's cabin as I approached and gave me a welcoming smile.

'Good afternoon, welcome to the Retreat.' He bent down to stroke Oscar's head. 'Both of you.'

He addressed me in Italian and I answered in the same language. Leo and I had already discussed my cover story in advance and when I trotted it out, the man appeared to accept it without demur.

'I'm staying with Mr Moretti and he told me I should come down and see the Retreat for myself. My girlfriend and I are coming to the Riviera next month and I thought it might be fun to bring her here for a few days. Neither of us has any experience of naturism but there's always a first time, isn't there?' Whether Anna and I would still be together by then was a different matter and, even if we were, I had no idea what her reaction might be if I were to suggest such a thing but, for the moment, it was a convenient ploy.

The man nodded and gave me a smile. 'Leo just called me, Signor Armstrong. Please come in and take a good look round.' He tapped his left breast. 'My name's Dario. Let me sort you out with a bracelet.' In response to my blank look, he explained. 'It's a smart bracelet. You need it to open the gate and for paying for food and drinks. I take an impression of guests' credit cards and they're automatically debited for each transaction.' I reached for my wallet but he stopped me. 'No need for that. Leo says you and your handsome dog are his guests.' Oscar wagged his tail at the compliment, but it might just have been because the guy was scratching his ears. He likes that.

He pointed to a small, white building a short distance ahead of me on the far side of the car park, just inside a sturdy wire fence taller than I was. 'The bracelet will open locker number six, where you leave your clothes. Let yourself in through the gate by pressing your bracelet against the illuminated panel alongside it. The gate will close automatically behind you. The lockers open and close the same way and are for the use of day visitors. Take all your clothes off and leave them in your locker and you're good to go. All right?'

That answered two of the questions that had been uppermost in my mind. I had been racking my brains trying to think of ways of carrying money, ranging from the impractical to the frankly physiologically uncomfortable, and the bracelet idea came as a considerable relief. The locker and the instruction to take all my clothes off and leave them in it was scarier, if expected. Muttering, 'In for a penny, in for a pound,' under my breath, I held out my arm and he secured a blue bracelet around my wrist. Doing my best to keep my tone light – mostly to hide my nerves – I pointed to it.

'Blue for a boy, pink for a girl?'

He gave me a grin. 'One of the advantages of a naturist retreat is that the genders don't normally need to be spelled out. All the bracelets here are blue.'

A practical question occurred to me. 'What about shoes? Is everybody barefoot?'

He shook his head. 'Not unless you want to be – and as long as the soles of your feet are up to it. Most of the paths are gravel so I always advise people to keep their shoes on, at least at first. Enjoy your time here at the Retreat. If you have any questions, just ask a member of staff. The bar and restaurant are just down there and there's a little shop and a games room in the clubhouse. We're all here to help.' He was probably reciting a well-practised script but he sounded genuine enough and I thanked him before heading into the camp.

I crossed the car park, noting a number of vehicles with foreign numberplates, until I came to the sturdy, iron, pedestrian gate. This was a good couple of metres high and the fence even higher. As Leo had said, the Retreat was clearly keen to keep unauthorised people out, and this made the possibility of Saturday night's death being the work of somebody from outside the camp improbable – unless there was an alternative entrance. As instructed, I pressed my wrist with the bracelet against the sensor on the gate post and the lock obediently clicked open. I went through and heard the gate close automatically behind me as I headed for the little white building marked *Visitors*.

I found myself in a simple room with a row of lockers against one wall and a long, wooden bench against the other. Feeling very self-conscious, even though the room was empty, I took off my clothes and hung them in locker number six. Somebody had helpfully – or maybe maliciously – positioned a full-length mirror on the end wall, next to a door marked with two cartoon characters in the buff, and I took a good look at myself before my foray into what was going to be a brand-new experience for me.

My face, legs and forearms were quite brown by now but the rest of me appeared terribly pale in comparison. My reflection in the mirror looked a bit like a choc-ice. It occurred to me that it might have been sensible to bring some sun cream and I decided I would do well to steer clear of too much direct sunlight for fear of ending up with sunburn in some delicate places.

To be honest, the thing that worried me most about my appearance was the fact that I was wearing shoes. Like most people, I was really only used to seeing myself naked in the bathroom or the bedroom, but seeing myself here with a pair of brown deck shoes on looked a bit weird. I removed my socks and stuck them in the locker and slipped my shoes back on again, but this didn't help much and I still felt decidedly odd. However, as the alternative would be to try and walk on gravel with bare feet, I knew I had no choice. Of course, Oscar was all right; his paws were tough enough for anything. Thought of Oscar reminded me of something I had been meaning to say so I glanced down at him and waved an admonitory finger.

'Now, listen, dog, you're going to meet a lot of new people and you're going to encounter a lot of new smells so, please, please try and avoid poking your nose where you shouldn't.'

He looked mildly offended but as I turned back towards the locker door I felt Oscar's nose nudge the back of my thigh. I'm just over six foot but I had a horrible feeling that other people whose centre of gravity was closer to the ground were going to have to watch out. I picked up my phone and notebook, trying to work out how best to carry them, before deciding to leave everything here for now. I slipped them back into the pocket of my shorts and closed the locker with my bracelet as instructed. Taking a deep breath, I reached for the door handle and the two of us stepped out into the brave new world of *La Torre Retreat*.

I emerged onto a gravel path bordered by a dense hedge of

rosemary bushes that curled over the path, forming a charming archway, effectively screening the Retreat from the view of anybody on the outside. The aroma of the little blue flowers was heady and the background buzz of industrious bees almost blanked out the chirping of sparrows. Emerging into the sunlight once again, I found myself in a flat, grassy area where I was confronted by the spectacle of half a dozen naked septuagenarians playing volleyball. As they leapt around remarkably athletically, I reached for Oscar's collar in case he chose to join in but, instead, all I got from him was a look of amazement that probably mirrored my own. One lady with snow-white hair who had to be nudging eighty gave me a little wave when she caught sight of me and I waved back, conscious that she was probably around the same age and build as my mum. One thing was for sure, you would have needed a tow truck to get my mother in here, but as my dad used to say, whatever floats your boat.

A little further along the path, I came to the bar/restaurant where I received a cheery smile from what I assumed to be a waitress who was carrying a tray. I had been wondering whether the staff would be fully clothed and I soon realised that this was not the case. She was probably only in her mid-twenties and I couldn't help noticing that she was a lot more physically appealing than the volleyball stars. Interestingly – and fortunately – I was far too overawed by my surroundings to feel any physical attraction and this served to allay another of my fears. The same couldn't be said for Oscar, whose tail immediately started wagging, and I had to grab him by the collar again to prevent him from following her retreating backside with his cold, wet nose and quite possibly making her drop the tray of drinks.

Determined to take things slow and to allow my overheated brain time to adjust to my new circumstances and surroundings, I took a seat at a table under a parasol, trying not to think too deeply about who might have been sitting here before me. I did my best to relax, making sure that Oscar lay down beside me, and I took a good look around. There were probably about twenty tables out here on the tiled terrace and four of the others were currently occupied. A little way from me was a group of four elderly men playing cards. Even from here I could see that the cards, when they smashed them down on the table with exclamations of satisfaction or frustration, weren't normal playing cards, but had unusual symbols of leaves and what looked like acorns on them. I don't speak much German but I recognised enough of the exclamations and expletives coming from that table to realise that these old boys had to be Germans, Austrians or Swiss.

Beyond them was a table where a deeply tanned, very blonde couple, maybe around the same age as Tricia, my daughter, were staring lovingly into each other's eyes. They looked fit and healthy and had deliberately taken a table without a sun umbrella, presumably so as to work on their tans. I had been warned numerous times by my ex-wife about the effects of the sun on fair skin and I hoped they knew what they were doing. Another table contained a couple who might have been in their late thirties and, by the look of their pink skin, they were relatively new arrivals. He was drinking beer and she had a glass of clear liquid that might have been water or it might have been gin and they weren't exchanging a word. I hoped this meant they were a happily married couple, content with their own company, but I somehow sensed hostility on that table. Memories of the final years of my marriage came to mind and I shook my head ruefully.

The other occupied table was more interesting – from a detective's point of view – as it contained a lone man with a half-empty bottle of red wine in front of him. He was probably around my age, wearing dark glasses, and although I couldn't see his eyes, it was pretty obvious he was studying his surroundings intently. And that included me. His head turned slightly in my direction and I felt him appraise me. I gave him a smile and a hint of a wave, got nothing in return and instinctively put him onto my nascent list of potential suspects.

'*Ciao*, what can I get you?'

I looked up to see the waitress at my shoulder. She was speaking English with a distinct Antipodean accent. There was a movement at my feet as Oscar stood up to greet her, his tail already wagging. I kept a very close eye on him in case he might decide to be a bit too friendly.

'Something non-alcoholic and refreshing, I think, please. Do you have a low-alcohol beer?'

She nodded. 'Of course. Would you like something to eat as well?'

Doing my best to keep my eyes only on her face, I decided to see if I could strike up a bit of conversation with her. 'No, thanks, I've just had lunch. It's the first time I've been here and I'm still just beginning to take it all in. What about you? Have you worked here long?'

'Every summer for the last five years. I love the place.'

'And what do you do for the rest of the time?'

'I go back to New Zealand and work in a naturist club near Wellington for the summer; that's our summer over there, I mean.'

'So you're a devotee of the naturist lifestyle?' I gave her a smile. 'Is that so as to save money on clothes?'

She smiled back. 'I just find it so liberating. You say you're new to the Retreat; are you new to naturism as well?'

I nodded. 'This is a first for me. It's taking a bit of getting used to.'

'Don't worry, it won't take long. I guarantee by this time

tomorrow, you won't even notice what you or any of the people around you are or aren't wearing.'

I hoped she was right but I had serious doubts.

She turned and went off to get my drink. I studiously avoided letting my eyes linger on her rear view and, instead, focused my attention on the direction of the pool. An immaculately trimmed hedge prevented me from seeing it from here, but shouts, happy screams and splashing indicated its location. I let my eyes roam around. Although the camp's hilltop surroundings on the other side of the perimeter fence were little more than barren, sun-scorched scrub, all the plants in here looked well cared for and the grass was a healthy green. No doubt there was a sophisticated sprinkler system to ensure that it remained lush and verdant throughout the hot, dry, Italian summers. Over to one side, I could see the roofs of a number of chalets and beyond them I knew from what I had seen from the top of the tower was where the tents and caravans started. The overall impression was of a meticulously maintained and spotlessly clean holiday resort and I felt sure that most, if not all, my companions here would feel the same way.

When the waitress returned with my beer and very kindly brought a bowl of water for Oscar, I asked her what her name was and she directed my attention to her left breast, which I had been studiously trying to ignore up till now. I spotted a tattoo on it indicating that her name was Sophie. She gave me a little grin. 'One of the disadvantages of not wearing a uniform is that it's hard to pin on a name badge.'

While Oscar slurped up his water, I gently broached the subject of the recent death. 'I heard that some guy was found floating in the pool at the weekend. Sounds like a horrible accident.'

Her smile vanished. 'It was awful. None of us could understand it; we still can't. Joseph was a really strong swimmer; he used to do twenty or thirty lengths every morning and again in the evening. The police said he was drunk, but I never saw him drink more than a glass or two of wine.'

The fact that she knew his first name was promising. 'Are you saying you think his death was suspicious?'

I saw her look around cautiously before answering. 'The police said it was an accident and I suppose they should know but, personally, I still can't get my head round it.'

'Did you know him well?'

'Pretty well; he was here for a few weeks last year as well, but he wasn't a very communicative sort of guy, although he was very good-looking and he always had a friendly word for the staff.' She shot me a little smile. 'Particularly the female staff, although he was always pleasant and polite.'

I reflected that if he, like Oscar, had had a way with the opposite sex, might this make the likelihood of his death being attributable to jealousy a bit more likely? I did my best to sound casual. 'Any female member of staff in particular?'

'Rita knew him best and she said he was a lovely man.'

'Rita...?'

'She's our personal trainer. She looks after the gym. Joseph was in there every day and she got to know him quite well.' Just for a moment, it looked as though she might be about to say more but instead, she just reached for Oscar's ears and stroked him. Even so, I filed the personal trainer's name away as potentially worthy of further investigation.

'And what about you, Sophie? Did you like him?'

'Definitely, like I say, he was a nice guy.' She lowered her voice. 'Unlike some...' I couldn't miss the fact that her eyes shifted momentarily to the man over to my right whose bottle of red wine was now three quarters empty. Fortunately, he was too far from us to notice or overhear.

I inclined my head in his direction. 'I suppose it's inevitable you get some awkward customers.'

'He's not so much awkward as odd. He's British and he knows I speak English, but all I get out of him are grunts. I sometimes wonder why people come on holiday when they're so obviously miserable. I suppose it's in an attempt to cheer themselves up, but it doesn't work for everybody. Also...' she lowered her voice even more '...he's a looker.'

She must have seen the bewilderment on my face as she hastily corrected herself. 'I don't mean he's good-looking, I mean he's one of those creepy men who just stares. He always wears those dark glasses so it's hard to see exactly where his eyes are focused, but Freddie and I both reckon he's a perv – we get them from time to time. It's rare to find them here at the Retreat but we both feel it, so it's not just me imagining things.'

'What's his name?'

'His surname's Griffiths, but I've no idea what his first name is. One thing's for sure, he's not short of money. That wine he's drinking is ten-year-old Barolo and he's staying in a luxury chalet all on his own.'

Maybe realising that she was talking out of turn, she bent away from me and gave Oscar a stroke while I hastily averted my eyes. Straightening up again, she gave me a little wave and went off. I added a notional asterisk alongside Mr Griffiths on my mental list of potential suspects – if, indeed, the death of Joseph Beck had been murder, rather than just an unfortunate accident.

6

WEDNESDAY AFTERNOON

After drinking my beer, I continued with my tour of inspection. A glance into the clubhouse revealed a pool table, a bar, a series of comfortable chairs and the little shop selling essentials like milk, bread, fruit and wine. There was only one person in here – an elderly gentleman reading a copy of the *Frankfurter Allgemeine Zeitung*. All I could see of him was his white hair and some of the bushiest eyebrows I had ever seen and a pair of bare legs protruding beneath the newspaper. To one side of the bar was a doorway marked *Uffici/Offices* and another looked as though it led to the kitchens. Back outside again, I headed for the pool. When I reached it, everywhere I looked, there were naked people standing, walking, swimming or lying on sun loungers. Something struck me as a little bit odd and it took me a moment or two before I realised that I couldn't see any children at all. Okay, so school holidays hadn't started here in Italy yet, but I found it strange that there weren't even any toddlers to be seen. Maybe this place was for adults only? I've always had a suspicious nature – as my ex-wife repeatedly told me – and I immediately found myself wondering if something more than naturism might be going on here. Had I inadvertently walked into a swingers' paradise?

A quick look around confirmed my original impression from the top of the tower that the majority of people here were older than me and, in many cases, ten or twenty years older than me. This made the chances of the place being something akin to Sodom and Gomorrah less likely, but I filed the thought away for future consideration. As a complete newcomer to naturism, I had no idea what drove people to holiday in the nude. If I was anything to go by, I certainly hadn't found it an erotic experience so far – very much the opposite – but maybe other people reacted differently. Certainly, if there had been lots of bed-swapping and hanky-panky going on, maybe the motivation for Joseph Beck's murder might have been good old-fashioned jealousy.

Unfortunately, while my attention was engaged in studying the humans around me, I momentarily forgot about my canine companion. There was a loud splash, followed by a few laughs, and I turned back to see a hairy black head emerge from the swimming pool with a big, toothy smile on his lips. Don't try and tell me Labradors can't smile. Oscar definitely can.

I hurried over to the water's edge and called him. He doggy-paddled towards me but showed no sign of wanting to get out of the water. Apart from anything else, I could see that this was going to be tricky anyway. The water here was deep and access was only by a stainless-steel ladder. I stood there helplessly for a few moments, wondering what to do, before realisation suddenly struck me that there was no reason why I shouldn't just jump in after him and help him out. All right, I didn't have a towel, but the hot sunshine would soon remedy that. Feeling strangely liberated, just as Sophie at the bar had said, I slipped off my shoes and jumped into the blissfully cool water.

When I surfaced, I was almost immediately greeted by a blast of canine breath from short range as my four-legged friend decided it would be a very good idea to try and climb onto my shoulders, almost drowning me in the process. I came up spluttering but then had a very pleasant couple of minutes playing about in the pool with him and savouring the refreshing feel of the water. Around us, half a dozen other swimmers smiled and fortunately, they appeared not to be bothered by the fact that their pool had been invaded by a Labrador. Finally, the two of us swam side by side the full length of the pool to the far end where a series of steps led upwards out of the water. I climbed out and Oscar followed, stopping to shake himself while I kept a safe distance – although it occurred to me as I did so that I wasn't wearing any clothes to protect – and then he trotted obligingly over to my side. I wagged my finger at him.

'We've had this conversation before, Oscar. Swimming pools aren't for dogs. Got that?'

'Don't worry, it doesn't matter. The filtration system can easily handle a few dog hairs.'

I looked up to see an athletic-looking young man wearing nothing but a red baseball cap with the word 'Lifeguard' written on it. He, too, had a New Zealand accent and I wondered whether he and Sophie from the bar might be friends, related to each other, or even in a relationship.

'Are you sure it's okay? I'm afraid my dog has a thing about water.'

'Yes, seriously, no problem. We like dogs around here, don't we?' He bent down to stroke Oscar's head. 'What's this guy's name?'

'He's Oscar and I'm Dan. We've just arrived.'

'I'm Billy. Good to meet you, Dan.' We shook hands and it felt bizarre to be performing such a formal act while both of us weren't wearing a stitch of clothing.

As he was looking and sounding communicative, I again brought up the subject of the recent death. 'It's surreal to think that only a few days ago, somebody was found floating in this very same pool, stone dead.'

He shook his head sadly. 'And he was such a nice guy, too.'

By this time, he had straightened up again but he carried on ruffling Oscar's ears. I kept a close eye on my dog just in case his nose might feel like investigating the lifeguard more intimately but, for now, he behaved himself and I returned my attention to the case. Here was another person who had known the victim well enough to claim to have liked him; this warranted further questioning. 'Sophie at the bar told me he was an accomplished swimmer. How come he drowned?'

Billy shrugged his shoulders helplessly and held out his hands, palms first, in disbelief. 'Beats me. I spend most of the day here under my umbrella.' He indicated a bright-red parasol behind him with a folding chair beneath it. 'I often saw him and he could swim like a fish – a damn sight better than me. He told me he swam for the university while he was at Oxford. He had a very stylish front crawl – a lot neater than mine.'

I noted those little snippets of information, particularly the fact that Beck would appear to have been well educated. What had his job been? I wondered. Had he been an academic? But an academic with a bullet wound to the stomach was surely hardly commonplace? I tried Billy again. 'Apparently, the police reckon he was drunk. Was that a common occurrence for him?'

'I was surprised when I heard that. He was a very fit guy and you could see he looked after his body. I can't imagine somebody like that poisoning himself with too much alcohol, but who knows? Maybe he had some bad news or something and he was drowning his sorrows.' He stopped and corrected himself. 'Sorry, that's an awful pun in the circumstances. It was very sad.'

A thought occurred to me. 'I heard that he probably died around midnight. Would there have been any lights on down here at that time?'

He shook his head. 'We have underwater lighting, which does a good job of illuminating the area, but that goes off every night at eleven. It would have been pretty dark down here.' He caught my eye for a moment. 'That's what makes it so weird, right?'

Conscious that I was fully exposed to the burning sun and of the water on my skin rapidly evaporating, I left him to his work, retrieved my shoes, and carried on with my tour, hugging any shade and carefully checking everything I came across, trying to memorise what I saw. It was clear that the hedge around the pool did a very good job of shielding that area from the sight of people outside the camp or at the main buildings. I could only just see the roof of the clubhouse and no trace of chalets or tents, so if somebody had deliberately assaulted and drowned Beck – particularly in the middle of the night when the lights had been turned off – it would have been quite easy to do it without being observed. But who and why?

A little way from the pool, I came upon a large, sail-shaped, white canvas awning, strung between four sturdy metal poles like a marquee without sides. It was open all the way round and in the shade beneath it, I could see a selection of exercise machines, weights and other apparatus. It came as no surprise to see that nobody was using these facilities – it really was a very hot afternoon – and there was only one figure visible inside, positioned on a yoga mat. I recognised the pose straight away. A few years ago, on the instructions of my ex-wife, I had dabbled with yoga, and the figure under the awning was unmistakably in the 'downward-facing dog' position. This involves forming an acute angle with the body with arms extended, face down and bottom in the air, and then holding it. Take my word for it, it's harder than it looks.

The bronzed bottom facing me as I approached presumably belonged to Rita, the personal trainer. Rather than address a naked bum, I circled around so as to approach her from the side and I saw her turn her face towards me, still holding the pose.

'*Ciao, sono Rita.*'

As she had addressed me in Italian, I replied in that language. '*Ciao*, I'm Dan. I've just arrived.'

She abandoned the stretch position and sat down, cross-legged, on the mat in front of me and held up her hand to shake mine. Oscar was delighted to find her down at his level and as he trotted across to greet her I gave her a few words of warning. 'I'm sorry about Oscar. He's just been in the pool so watch out.'

'*Ciao*, Oscar, what a handsome dog you are!' Soggy or not, she reached out and hugged him, which started his tail wagging enthusiastically. Finally releasing him from her embrace, she subjected me to a close examination, eyeing me up and down like a piece of meat on a slab. I could feel my cheeks – and a few other parts of my body – flush, but she hastened to reassure me. 'I can see you look after your body. Bravo! Are you going to join us here in the fitness centre?'

Doing my best to look as if chatting to naked women was commonplace for me, I hedged my bets. 'I'm not sure how long I'm here for, but I'll think about it – as long as it doesn't get any hotter. Do you have many clients here at the gym?'

'Regulars, only three or four at the moment, but people drop in and out, normally in the mornings or evenings when it's not so hot.'

'That makes sense. The others have been telling me about the tragic death of one of your clients the other day. That must have been terrible.'

An unmistakable wave of emotion swept across her face. 'It was awful.' Her voice tailed away and it was clear that she was still upset. I gave her a few moments and then returned to the subject of the victim.

'Did you know him well?'

From what Sophie had told me, I had been expecting her to nod and agree but, instead, a haunted expression appeared on her face.

'Reasonably well. He was a regular here at the gym.' The expression was definitely tinged with caution now, and I had the feeling that she was weighing her words carefully. 'Guests don't tend to stay for long and he'd only been here for a couple of weeks but, yes, I suppose I knew him quite well.'

My detective antennae started twitching. The others had said this had been his second year here. Of course, Rita might not have been working here then or Sophie might have been mistaken, but I definitely got the impression that Rita was trying to play down any involvement she might have had with the dead man. Whether this was because of grief or a sense of impropriety or for some other reason remained unclear for now, but I added this to my developing mental list of noteworthy points. Maybe fraternisation between staff and guests was frowned upon or maybe there was another reason for her reticence.

Like the wedding ring on her left hand for instance.

After chatting for a little longer but without obtaining any more information about the victim, I spent the next hour wandering around the camp, checking out the toilet and shower blocks, the mini golf course and the grassy area where the tents were pitched. A few mainly elderly people were sitting in the shade and most gave me at least a friendly smile, if not an actual greeting. As always, Oscar proved to be an excellent icebreaker and ambassador. In the course of the hour, I probably spoke briefly to seven or eight other people – mainly northern Europeans – but discovered nobody who claimed to have known the victim well until I reached the last of the three rather swish-looking 'luxury' chalets. Unlike the other chalets, these were larger and made of masonry with flat roofs, on which I could see air-conditioning units. This one had a little piece of private garden to the front, surrounded by flower beds ablaze with colour. In the shade of a wooden pergola swathed in luxuriant vines were two easy chairs and on one of them there was a woman, probably in her late forties, while on the other there was a black miniature poodle. From its grey jowls, it was pretty clear it was no longer in the first flush of youth and when it saw Oscar, it bared its upper lip to show its teeth and produced a menacing growl – insofar as something little bigger than a pussycat can sound menacing.

Oscar is essentially a pacific, friendly dog, whether dealing with humans or other animals – apart from squirrels – and he stopped in surprise and gave me a questioning look, as much as to say, *What's his problem?* The woman alongside the poodle reached over and tapped it on the nose with a manicured finger.

'Rudolph, behave yourself.' Her accent was educated middle England and if it hadn't been for the word *Peace* tattooed on her left breast and *Love* tattooed on the other one, she could have been a country schoolmarm. Mind you, I have no direct personal experience of schoolmarms and their choice of tattoos. Maybe this was par for the course in certain literary circles. She returned her attention to me and gave me a smile.

'Tuo cane bello.'

Although not strictly grammatically correct, I was impressed that she had taken the trouble to attempt to address me in the language of the country in which she now found herself. I stopped, smiled back, and replied in English.

'Oscar thanks you for the compliment. Sorry your dog doesn't feel the same way about him.'

'Oh, don't worry about Rudolph. He's hot and it makes him grumpy. I haven't seen you around before. I'm Melinda. Are you new?'

I told her my name was Dan and gave her my cover story about maybe coming back with Anna.

'Hello, Dan. I'm sure your girlfriend will love it here. Also, if you're interested, Kim and I've found a little beach down on the coast, which is open to naturists. I still don't think you can beat swimming in the sea as nature intended.'

I was quick to capitalise on the opening she'd given me. 'Talking of swimming, I've just been chatting to the lifeguard and he told me there was a tragic death here the other day.'

A more serious expression appeared on her face and she nodded. 'Yes, it was very sad. Joseph was a nice man.'

Something in her tone struck me as questionable. Over the years, both in my professional and my personal life, I've come to realise that the adjective 'nice' can carry a multitude of nuances. A nice day's a nice day, but when you give somebody a present they deem unsatisfactory, this can often be awarded the descriptor 'nice' as thinly veiled criticism. Might this mean that Melinda hadn't liked the victim or was I reading something into her choice of words that wasn't there? She and the victim were both about the same age and the same nationality. Could it be that she, too, had found Mr Beck appealing but that he had turned her down? Alternatively, maybe he hadn't turned her down but it had all ended badly? Either way, what might her partner have had to say about that? This wasn't something I could ask easily but, again, I filed it away for future reference.

Just then, the door of the chalet opened and a tall, elegant woman emerged, ducking her head as she came out. I realised that this was probably Kim. She had to be ten or fifteen years younger than Melinda, very slim and remarkably beautiful, with sculpted features and a mane of lush, dark hair. Oscar immediately started wagging his tail and I could see why. Kim could have come straight out of the pages of *Vogue*. Melinda made the introductions.

'Kim, this is Dan. He's just arrived.'

Kim gave me a little wave of the fingers and an attempt at a smile but I could see that she wasn't looking too cheerful so I hastily took my leave and left. I couldn't help wondering why she was looking unhappy. Might that have been grief or even guilt, or something completely different?

I stopped off back at the clubhouse to ask if I could talk to the manager and was greeted with the information that he and Freddie, the catering manager, had gone to Imperia but would be back later on. In consequence, I decided to return to Leo at the tower.

As I walked back towards the changing rooms, I worked out that I had probably seen, or at least glimpsed, most of the fifty-six people plus staff, but I had spoken very briefly to only about a dozen of them. Even so, I had a feeling that it wouldn't take long for the bush telegraph to spread the news that the new arrival with the big, black dog had been asking questions about the death of Joseph Beck and I wondered what results – if any – this might produce. Might this flush somebody out of the woodwork?

7

WEDNESDAY LATE AFTERNOON

It felt almost strange to put my clothes on again. As I walked out of the gate and back towards the tower, I reflected on my first experience of naturism. All in all, it hadn't been as terrifying as I had thought and, although I felt sure I would still be very conscious of my nakedness and that of everybody else for some time to come, I was beginning to understand what Sophie had meant about it feeling liberating. For a moment, I seriously considered suggesting to Anna that we come here, but I knew that was a decision I was going to have to leave to her. Needless to say, thought of Anna risked spiralling me into introspection and, at least for now, I had a job to do, so I did my best to ignore my own personal problems and concentrate on what had happened here on Saturday night. Besides, even if Anna were to accept my apologies and came back to the Riviera with me in two weeks' time, might there still be a murderer around? Bringing her here in those circumstances wouldn't be a very smart move.

I let myself in through the front door of the tower and went up to the first floor, where I found Leo sitting on one of the sofas, reading a book. As I came in, he held it up towards me.

'Look familiar, Dan? *Death Amid the Vines*. Bianca left it for me and told me I'd enjoy it. She was right.' He dropped the book down on the sofa beside him. 'Find out anything?'

'Not a lot, except that most of the people who admitted to knowing him, or at least having met him, said he was a nice guy. He was also apparently a good-looking guy and maybe a bit of a charmer. I met one of the guests who might or might not have had a thing for him, and Rita in the gym might have been involved with him as well, but I might be wrong. Out of interest, how long has she worked here?'

'Since we opened, five years ago.'

'And is she married?'

'Yes, to Dario on the main gate.'

'Happily married?'

'Very, as far as I know, but I imagine the girls at the café would know more. Why, surely you don't think he might have killed Beck, do you? Dario wouldn't hurt a fly, I'm sure.'

'I'm just trying to run through all possible scenarios. I have to keep a completely open mind for now until I can start eliminating people from my inquiries. What I really need is the police report, particularly the pathologist's report, but, of course, I'm no longer on the force and I'm not even Italian, so there's no way that's going to happen. I'll go back a bit later on and speak to the manager and the catering manager and then I'll have dinner at the Tower Restaurant in the hope of picking up something useful. I'll go back tomorrow as well in the hope of a breakthrough, but there's a limit to what I can achieve in an informal capacity.'

Leo was no fool. 'I get what you're saying, Dan. It's good of you to warn me that there's a chance you won't be able to add anything more, but at least I'll have the satisfaction of knowing that I tried. Just do your best. I know you will.'

'My main concern for now is to find a concrete piece of

evidence that points away from it just being an accident. All I've got so far is that the guy was a powerful swimmer and allegedly he didn't drink much, which makes the official story less credible, but that still doesn't prove anything.' I looked at my watch. 'It's almost six. I should just about have time to drive down to the town to buy myself a pair of flip-flops. Want to come along?'

I was really only being polite but, to my surprise, he hauled himself to his feet. 'I know what I'd like and I reckon you'd like one as well. Why don't I take you to the best ice-cream shop on the Ligurian coast? Sound good?'

That sounded very good. After I'd helped myself to a big glass of water and given Oscar a good long drink, we went downstairs and climbed into the van. I drove very carefully back down the steep hill, fortunately without meeting any other vehicles on the hairpin bends, and followed the main road down the valley, past the motorway entrance, and into the little seaside resort of San Clemente Spiaggia. There was an old church on a little promontory at one end of the town with no more than a dozen old houses clustered around it and a little harbour below it but, apart from that, almost all the buildings were relatively modern, probably dating back to the sixties or seventies, and few of any great aesthetic value. Still, it had a cheery, holiday feel, even if it lacked the historic elegance of Tuscany.

There was an old-fashioned promenade lined with palm trees overlooking a fine sandy beach, but the overall impression was somewhat marred by the railway line running tight alongside it. As we drove parallel to the beach, a passenger train came past and I felt sure guests in the seafront hotels who had opted for rooms with a sea view hadn't bargained on also occupying a perfect trainspotting position. Or maybe they had. My old superintendent at Scotland Yard used to spend thousands every year going on steam trains all over Europe. I could never see the attraction, but at least those trips got him off my back for a few weeks so I hadn't complained.

In true Italian tradition, the beach here at San Clemente Spiaggia had been carved up into lots of different *bagni*, distinguishable by their clusters of different-coloured parasols, arranged with geometric precision, where beachgoers pay for the use of sunbeds, an umbrella and a meticulously raked stretch of sand down to the water. Most of these bathing establishments also offer changing rooms and showers and quite a few have a bar or even restaurant facilities. It's certainly a far cry from a couple of towels on the windswept beach at Margate where I had enjoyed occasional day trips as a kid. I also couldn't help noticing signs indicating that dogs were not permitted on the beach but, fortunately, I now knew that Oscar's lust for water could be catered for in the Retreat pool.

People were coming away from the beach by this time and I was easily able to find a parking space in the main street, just one row of buildings back from the promenade. Here I almost immediately found a shop where I was able to buy a pair of skin-coloured flip-flops that would, I felt sure, look less inappropriate than my brown leather shoes. Once I had made my purchase, Leo led me back to the seafront and we walked along to his favourite gelateria.

A huge open fridge ran the length of the shop, crammed with tubs of ice cream. I counted no fewer than thirty-two different flavours ranging from liquorice to meringue, passing through passion fruit and lurid-blue bubble gum on the way to salted caramel. I watched as Leo ordered himself a mixture of pistachio, dark chocolate and coconut before I decided to play safe and asked for strawberry, white chocolate and meringue. I was just about to go to the till when the woman behind the counter pointed at Oscar and I thought she was going to say I shouldn't have brought him in, but instead she had a suggestion. 'Would your dog like to try our special ice cream for dogs?'

No offer of food is ever refused by my Labrador and I had no hesitation in saying yes on his behalf. I glanced down at him and, for a moment, I swear I saw him nod his head in agreement. His ice cream in fact turned out to be a pink iced lolly on a stick and I was surprised to hear that the flavour was 'apple'. I don't know what I'd been expecting – beef, rabbit, or recently exhumed bone maybe – but it quite evidently appealed to Oscar's taste buds. Although the idea was for me to hold it for him to gradually lick while I ate my own bowl of ice cream, within a very short space of time, he had broken off chunks, chewed them, swallowed them and then returned to devour the rest. The ice-cream seller had told me it would last for ten to fifteen minutes. Oscar wolfed it down in barely two and then spent five minutes gnawing the stick until that was little more than matchwood. He definitely likes his food but nobody could mistake him for an epicurean.

It came as no surprise to find that Leo insisted on paying and he and I took considerably more time over our own ice creams, sitting at a table outside on the pavement in the shade of a colourful awning. As we did so, I ran through some of the various scenarios that had occurred to me as possibly having provided a motive for murder.

'In the first instance, assuming it wasn't simple misadventure, there's always the possibility of a woman being involved. In my experience, sex, jealousy, passion and lust can all easily develop into reasons to kill. He was a good-looking guy and according to Sophie in the restaurant, he had a way with women. And there are certainly some good-looking women at the Retreat.'

Leo nodded his head and asked the obvious question. 'Yeah, but which woman?'

'I suppose one of the women I saw this afternoon might have

been, if not the perpetrator of the assault, at least the catalyst behind it. Maybe the personal trainer with the wedding ring, the Englishwoman with the grumpy dog or even her stunning companion who looked so unhappy, or one of the other women at the bar or lying by the pool? Notionally removing anybody over retirement age from the equation – although anything's possible – I still reckon that probably leaves us with at least fifteen women of the right sort of age. Statistically, let's say at least half of them could have appealed to a man in his mid to late forties. Interviewing all of them would take a lot of time and, without a legal mandate, I can't see that happening very easily. I can't force them to answer my questions.'

'And if it wasn't a woman?'

'The impression I've got is that Beck was a ladies' man – or at least, they seemed to have been drawn to him. If the killer was a man, the most likely suspect has to be one connected with one of the women – a jealous husband, boyfriend, lover, who knows? Alternatively, if he was killed by a woman, she might have been jealous of one of the others. Of course, it might not be a crime of passion. Another popular motive for committing murder is money, or at least personal gain in some shape or form. Without knowledge of Beck's financial status, his job or anything about his background, that's just conjecture, as are any of the other possible motives. The guy had a scar on his abdomen that could have been caused by a bullet. Does that mean somebody already tried and failed to kill him for some reason and that same person came back to try again? Does it mean Beck did a dangerous job, like being a soldier or, less laudably, maybe he belonged to the criminal fraternity? Who knows? Maybe he was killed because of something he knew, something he did or, of course, there's always the possibility that he was killed by mistake or, as the police believe, by accident.' I gave Leo a helpless look. 'Take your pick.

All options remain on the table, but one thing's for sure, I need to find out all I can about Joseph Beck. Is there anything else about him you haven't told me? Anything you might have forgotten?'

I kept my eyes on his face as I waited for an answer and, once again, I felt sure I spotted uncertainty, hesitation and maybe a guilty conscience. If he had been sitting in front of me in an interview room, I would have leant on him harder, but I was conscious that he was not only my current employer but also my landlord so I sat back until he finally spoke.

'No, I don't think so, but you should ask Bianca when she comes back on Friday.'

Even Oscar must have been able to hear the insincerity in his voice. One thing was certain: when it came to telling lies, his daughter was a whole lot more accomplished than he was.

When we got back up to the tower, the first thing I did was to check my phone again. Still no reply from Anna. Taking a big breath, I called her. The phone rang half a dozen times and then went to voicemail. For a moment, I was tempted to hang up immediately but then I managed to rally a certain amount of gumption. 'Hi, Anna. Look, you just need to know that I'm really sorry for last night. I know it might have looked as though I was getting cold feet as far as our relationship's concerned, but that's not true and I'll do whatever it takes. I love you. Please call me.'

And that was the best I could come up with on the spur of the moment.

Doing my best to ignore my own problems, I spent half an hour checking through the documents Leo had sent to my laptop. I pulled out my notebook and copied down the names of the seven Brits at the camp: Oliver and Fleur Harcourt, Jeremy Smith and Lorraine Hickson, Melinda Barker and Kim Russell and one man travelling alone. This was Owen Griffiths from Swansea, barely a few months older than me at fifty-seven. Apart from him, there were two other single men at the Retreat: a German called Klaus Schinken, age sixty-five, and a forty-two-year-old Czech called Adam Novotny. Italians were in a minority. As I had suspected, most of the guests were northern Europeans, principally Germans. From what Sophie had said, the creepy guy with the dark glasses sitting on his own had to be Owen Griffiths and I underlined his name on my list.

If I'd been running the investigation with the full resources of the Metropolitan Police behind me, I would have ordered a careful background investigation of the victim and then cross-referenced it with the other guests in the hope of finding points that overlapped, whether professionally, personally, or simply occasions on which they had been in the same place at the same time. However, given that the local police had taken barely a day to decide it had been an accident, I felt it unlikely that anything like this would have been set in train.

I studied the scanned copy of the victim's passport closely. This was only the page with the photo and the bare minimum details so I had no way of knowing what visas or entry and exit stamps to interesting countries there might have been on the inside pages. I paid special attention to his face but, like with most passport photos, which have to be studiously expressionless, it was hard to get a feel for the man. He had been forty-six but he looked younger. He had a square jaw and close-cropped, fair hair and I had to agree that he was a good-looking guy. I noticed that the entry under Place of Birth was Chemnitz. This certainly didn't sound very English and a quick check on the Internet revealed that Chemnitz was in fact in Germany. Maybe he was originally German or had lived there for a period, which would account for his fluency in the language.

As far as the passport itself was concerned, it looked convincing enough, but there are some very good forgeries going around these days. Of course, criminals can always go down the old tried and tested route of assuming the identity of somebody now deceased who would have been of a similar age to their own, had they lived. By applying for a copy of that person's birth certificate, they can then try to assume his or her identity. It's a time-consuming process but it still works, even though more checks and balances have been introduced by the Passport Office over the past few years.

Just in case, I emailed a copy of the page to my friend and former colleague at Scotland Yard, Inspector Paul Wilson, apologising for imposing on his goodwill and begging a favour. I asked if he could do a check on Beck's identity, the validity of his passport and, if possible, dig up any information on his background or occupation. I knew it was a long shot, not least because realistically I had less than forty-eight hours before I would be on my way back to Florence.

I closed the laptop and sat there for a moment or two, watching Oscar stretched out at my feet, no doubt dreaming of apple-flavoured ice lollies now as well as squirrels. The question I asked myself was quite simply: did I seriously believe that Beck had been murdered or had it been an accident as decided by the police? It didn't take me long to realise that, in spite of a lack of evidence or indeed much general information, something deep down inside me – call it an old copper's hunch – was tending to make me think that maybe there had been something suspicious about the death after all.

Proving it, of course, was going to be a whole different kettle of fish.

8

WEDNESDAY EVENING

It felt strange – but not totally alien this time – to be stripping off rather than dressing up for dinner. Slipping on my new flip-flops, I locked my clothes in locker number six and walked down the path to the Tower bar/restaurant at just after half past eight. As I did so, a thought occurred to me. Dario on the gate had told me the lockers were for the use of 'day visitors'. Had there been any of these at the Retreat on the day of the murder? For that matter, had Bianca Moretti been among their number? Her father had told me that she was a regular visitor to the Retreat so had she been there that night? I needed to check.

The sun was low on the horizon by now and the temperature had dropped a few degrees, but even without a stitch of clothing, there was no question of my feeling cold. I couldn't help wondering how committed naturists managed during a particularly cold, wet spell. Was there a special bad weather dispensation that allowed them to cover up to avoid hypothermia? That, at least, was not a problem that needed to trouble me today.

The tables on the terrace were now almost all occupied, but I was able to find a centrally positioned one close to the back wall from where I should hopefully be able to keep my eyes on as many of the guests as possible. The first thing I noticed was that Owen Griffiths, the sinister man with the shades, was still seated in the exact same spot as before. Whether he had gone away and subsequently returned, or whether he just hadn't moved from his seat, remained unclear. He still had his sunglasses on and I wondered how much of his food he could see as the light dwindled and the shadows deepened. I was now sitting parallel to him, separated by an empty table and one with a couple of French pensioners on it, and it occurred to me that just as I had selected this position as being in the best place to give me an all-round view, the same quite possibly applied to him, particularly after what Sophie had said about him potentially being a voyeur.

As I scanned the tables, I spotted Love and Peace Melinda sitting opposite stick-thin Kim while the head of the grumpy poodle suddenly popped up on a third chair between the two of them, staring malevolently at Oscar. Melinda gave me a little smile when she saw me but the beautiful Kim barely reacted. She was either grieving, unhappy, or angry about something. Alternatively, maybe she just didn't wave at strange men. Whatever it was, her mood was casting its own shadows across her perfect features.

I recognised a few of the other faces from my walkabout this afternoon and mentally checked off some of the others from the list Leo had sent me. As before, my current lack of pockets meant that I hadn't brought the list, my phone or even my notepad and I began to notice that most of the people around me had bags of some description for their valuables. Maybe I should do the same. Still, even without my list, I gradually managed to pigeon-hole most of those around me by nationality if not by name.

The four elderly German-speaking men who had been playing cards earlier now occupied four separate tables with their respective wives, while the opposing volleyball players were all seated together around one big table. To my untrained ear, they appeared to be speaking one of the Scandinavian languages. As before, there was a total absence of children and I made a mental note to query this when I had the chance to talk to one of the staff. As it happened, the opportunity to do so very quickly presented itself. A woman with bright-pink hair suddenly materialised at my side, a tray in her hands. From this, she removed a printed menu and handed it to me.

'Good evening. You must be Leo's friend from Florence. I'm Freddie.' She spoke to me in Italian so I replied in kind.

'I'm pleased to meet you, Freddie. I'm Dan and this is Oscar. You're the catering manager, aren't you?' By this time, Oscar was on his feet, cold, wet nose poised, and I reached out to give him a gentle tap on the head. 'You just behave yourself, dog. If you do, there may be some food in it for you.'

The threat – and the offer – did the trick and he sat back down primly and adopted his 'faithful companion' look. Freddie bent down to ruffle his ears and the end of his tail wagged, but thankfully he resisted the temptation to jump to his feet and start pawing her.

'Are you eating, Dan?'

'Definitely. What would you recommend?'

'We've just brought a load of fresh seafood back from Imperia and the chef makes a really good *fritto misto*. How does that sound?'

I certainly wouldn't describe myself as a foodie but there are some dishes that I really love, and this traditional Italian mix of whitebait, octopus, squid rings, prawns and anything else that has been brought in with the day's catch has always been one of my favourites. I agreed readily and asked for a tiny taster of something first and left the choice of antipasti up to her. After my huge plate of pasta at lunchtime, I was hungry, but not starving. Conscious that Leo was paying for this, I just asked for a small carafe of white wine but when Sophie, the waitress, arrived a minute or two later with a basket of bread and a bottle of water, she also put a bottle of white wine on the table in front of me and proceeded to open it, ignoring my objections.

'This is Leo's favourite. He said you have to try it; he's sure you'll like it.'

The label indicated that this was a wine called Pigato, which was a new one on me, and it was made by a producer only a few kilometres away from here. Pulling out the cork, Sophie half-filled my glass and waited while I tasted it. It was cold, it was crisp, it was dry and it was beautifully fruity. I nodded in approval.

'Leo has very good taste. This is excellent. Thanks a lot.'

She didn't immediately walk away and I sensed that she had something on her mind. I lowered my voice and gave her an enquiring glance. 'All well?'

She leant closer to me as she topped up my glass and answered in little more than a whisper. 'Half an hour ago, Mr Griffiths, the creepy guy, spoke to me.'

'I thought you said he only grunted.'

'That's right, but this time he actually spoke... proper words. I was surprised to hear him talking but I was even more surprised by what he said.'

'And that was...?'

'It was the strangest thing. He said, "I see you've got a detective on the case now. I'm not surprised. It was murder, you know." That was all he said.'

I had half been expecting people to start suspecting my real reason for being here sooner or later, but hearing somebody else so certain that Beck's death had been murder made me sit up and take notice. What, I wondered, was he basing this assertion on and was it maybe even shared by other people here? I had a feeling I was probably going to have to sit down and interview fifty-six people in the morning. 'Did you ask him what he meant?'

She shook her head. 'To be honest, I was so surprised to hear him come out with something comprehensible that I just gave him his drink, mumbled something, and then went off. I presume he was referring to you. You are a detective, aren't you?'

'Is that what Leo told you?'

'Not in so many words. He said you were a friend with an inquisitive streak. It doesn't take much to put two and two together.'

I was still digesting what Griffiths had said, but I paused for thought before deciding that it probably wouldn't do any harm to come clean and admit why I was here. As I was so short of clues, there was the chance that my presence alone might prompt the perpetrator into some kind of reaction. I nodded.

'Yes. I used to be in the police back in the UK, but now I'm a private investigator based here in Italy. It's interesting what that guy said to you about it having been murder. That's what Leo thinks as well.'

'But who... why...?' Her voice tailed off helplessly.

'That's what I'm hoping to find out. Thanks a lot for the information. If anything else occurs to you or to any of the other staff members, I'll be only too pleased to hear. Do, please, spread the word.'

She picked up her tray and headed off, leaving me mulling over what she had just told me. Did the man with the glasses have evidence to back up his assertion? If so, then I needed to hear it. As soon as I could, I knew I wanted to speak to him, but at that moment, Freddie arrived with my starter. I had only asked for something small but I found myself presented with a little pot of olives and sun-dried tomatoes in extra virgin olive oil and an unusual thin yellow pancake sort of thing that she told me was made of chickpea flour. In spite of its unprepossessing appearance, it turned out to be incredible. She said this was a local speciality called *farinata*. I've never been terribly keen on lentils or the like but this was totally different from anything I had had elsewhere and I loved it. It had a distinct flavour of rosemary and, although the appearance was uninspiring, the taste was unique and delightful, the form and texture not dissimilar to a French crêpe.

As I ate, I felt eyes on me and looked up from time to time to intercept curious glances from some of the other tables. Presumably, the bush telegraph had disseminated the information that I was asking questions about the death of Joseph Beck. I tried to work out whether any of my fellow diners were exhibiting anything more than idle curiosity, but I couldn't identify anybody looking defensive, aggressive or guilty.

After finishing my *farinata*, I settled back to nibble the olives and sip the excellent white wine, my eyes still roaming around the terrace. The general mood around me was cheerful and, with food like this, I didn't blame them. It took me a minute or two before the realisation suddenly dawned on me that I hadn't even noticed that everybody was naked. Maybe Sophie was right and I was shedding my inhibitions.

When the *fritto misto* appeared, I devoted myself to it while my dog produced a series of lugubrious sighs from beneath the table, desperately trying to convince me that he was in the latter stages of starvation. Knowing his appetite of old, I hardened my heart and dug in. The mixture of seafood was absolutely excellent, lightly dusted with flour and quickly fried, served on a silver platter with absorbent brown paper underneath to soak up any residual oil. This definitely had to rank among the top two or three *fritti misti* I had ever eaten, and I'm sure Oscar agreed. I handed him down a couple of prawn heads, a breadstick and a little piece of octopus just to keep him happy and, as ever, they disappeared in an instant.

Sophie persuaded me to have a panna cotta with caramelised apricots afterwards and I couldn't fault that either. I could see now why Leo's chain of restaurants in New York had made him a wealthy man. I felt sure that if he were to set up a restaurant down at the seaside, he would have no shortage of clients. Finally, feeling full, I stretched my legs and ordered an espresso. This was brought to me by the pink-haired catering manager and she stopped to chat. It was immediately clear that she also knew why I was here.

'So you think it was murder?'

I decided to be frank. 'I must admit that I'm beginning to think it might have been, but it's little more than a hunch for now. What I need is something concrete, some proof. Is there anything you can tell me about the victim?'

Many of the tables had already emptied as people who had started eating before me disappeared back to their accommodation and I saw that the French couple alongside me were in the process of making a move as well. This very neatly gave us freedom to talk without risk of being overheard. Freddie pulled out a chair and sat down opposite me.

'I can't tell you much except for the fact that I wouldn't be surprised if he was having a bit of a fling with Kim... you know, the model.'

This was interesting. By the look of it, there must have been a fifteen- or twenty-year age gap between Beck and her. I had instinctively been considering her older friend, Melinda, as more likely to have paired up with the victim, so I had to do a bit of rethinking. 'Kim's a model?'

Freddie nodded. 'Kim Russell is a very well-known model. I recognised her at once. Her photos appear in all the fashion magazines.'

'I'm afraid I don't read a lot of those. She *is* very beautiful, though. And you think she might have been hooking up with Joseph Beck?'

'They were very circumspect about it, but Billy down at the pool said he saw them together a few times.'

'Together how?'

'Just chatting, I think, but he said they looked close, if you know what I mean.'

Another thought occurred to me. 'Surely if she's famous and she's walking around in the nude, wouldn't she have been afraid of her photos being leaked to the media?'

'That's why she's come here to us. We have a strict no-camera rule. Our mantra is: no clothes, no kids, no cameras. We're very discreet. This is a place where adults can relax without fear of unpleasant distractions or revelations.' She lowered her voice. 'Last week, we had a very famous couple of American actors here.'

'And nobody breaks the rules? Surely most people have phones with cameras these days.'

'If anybody's caught breaking the rules, they're banned, not only from this retreat but from all the others in the European network to which we belong. It happens every now and then but it's far less common than you might think.'

I decided I'd better voice my suspicions. 'Given that this place is adults-only, might there be a certain amount of...?' I was unfamiliar with the Italian for 'swinging' so I improvised. 'Might there have been a lot of sexual misconduct going on?'

She answered immediately, sounding defensive. 'Certainly nothing condoned by the management. I'm sure there's a certain amount of holiday romance, but we wouldn't want to get a reputation for being one of *those* sorts of places.' There was distinct disapproval in her voice now. 'We have a good name and we're very keen to maintain that.'

'And what about intimate relations between staff and guests? Does that happen?'

'Again, it's frowned on although we can't completely ban it. In fact, two years ago Clara, one of our waitresses, fell in love with a Swedish man and they're now happily married and living in Stockholm. Like I say, it can happen, but we don't encourage it.'

I wondered if this might be another reason why Rita at the gym had been so reticent when asked about her relations with the victim, but I avoided asking Freddie about it – for now.

'And Bianca, Leo Moretti's daughter, would she have known Joseph Beck?'

Freddie had to stop and think for a moment. 'I'm sure she knew him, the same way most of us did. To be completely honest, he was a very good-looking guy, but I never saw her looking particularly intimate with him.'

'Does she have a boyfriend?'

'You'd have to ask her that, but I've never seen her with anybody. Maybe there's somebody back in England. She told me she's doing a university course and she's trying to concentrate on that.'

'Can you remember if she was here last Saturday, when Joseph Beck died?'

'I'm afraid I can't remember. Maybe Sophie might know.'

'Coming back to Kim, the model, how about Melinda, the woman Kim's sharing with? What does she do?'

'Melinda Barker's very famous in her own right as well. Have you ever heard of CGFC, the Chelsea Global Fashion Company?' I shook my head and she grinned. 'Fashion's not your specialist subject, is it? Anyway, they're a very upmarket fashion house with branches all over the world, and she owns it.' She glanced over her shoulder to check that Melinda and Kim had already left. 'She's a regular here. She brings a different beautiful girl every year.' She gave me a hint of a wink.

I gave this some thought. What if the budding relationship between the victim and the model had sparked jealousy? I wondered how Melinda would have taken the news if she had found out, or whether there might have been somebody else who had taken exception to this liaison. I filed this information away for now, my thoughts returning to the allegedly creepy Mr Owen Griffiths. As I did so, I glanced across to check that he was still at his table and was annoyed to see it now empty. Suppressing an expletive, I asked Freddie for her opinion of him and I saw her expression sour.

'All he ever does is sit at that table and stare. I always keep an eye on him when I'm passing in case he tries taking any sneaky pictures. His phone's permanently on the table in front of him but, so far, there's no sign he's doing anything like that, but he's a bit creepy.' She looked up at me and shrugged her shoulders. 'We get them from time to time. All we can do is keep a close eye on him. If he crosses the line, he'll be out on his ear. With no refund. Everybody signs a conduct contract before coming here, agreeing to the terms and conditions, so they know the risks. Hopefully, he'll just restrict himself to looking and nothing more.'

At that moment, we were joined by a man with one of the hairiest chests – not to mention the rest of him – I had ever seen. I was sure there had to be balder grizzly bears out there than this guy. Still, he looked a whole lot friendlier than the average grizzly bear and Oscar immediately sprang to his feet, tail wagging. Of course, this might have been because he'd mistaken the man for a fellow black Labrador, but maybe I was just being ungenerous. The new arrival smiled at me and held out his hand.

'Hi, I'm George, I'm the manager. You must be Dan.' He addressed me in excellent English.

Freddie jumped to her feet and pointed to her seat. 'Sit down, George, I need to go and see if Luigi needs a hand in the kitchen.'

The manager shook hands with me and then sat down. Glancing around warily, he leant forward across the table. 'Any news?'

I shook my head. 'Nothing concrete, but I'm definitely beginning to feel that the police may have got it wrong.'

An expression of satisfaction crossed his face. 'That's what I told them the other day, but they wouldn't believe me.'

'If it was murder, do you have any suspects in mind? As far as opportunity's concerned, I suppose more or less anybody could have met the victim down at the pool and bashed him over the head. As for means, we need to know whether we're looking for a blunt object, a piece of wood, a piece of metal or some other improvised club or whether the headwound was really inflicted by a trip and a fall. The pathologist's report would cover all that, but of course I can't get sight of it. And then there's the question of motive. Any ideas?'

'I wouldn't be surprised if there was a woman involved. You could tell as soon as you looked at him that Joseph was a ladies' man. And that can lead to jealousy or worse.'

'Indeed. Any specific woman?'

'You'd better ask Freddie or Sophie; they're better at sniffing out that sort of thing than I am.' He hesitated. 'But I saw him with Kim, the model, one evening and I remember thinking that they were looking comfortable together, maybe more than comfortable.'

That confirmed what Freddie had said. 'There's a guy called

Owen Griffiths who looks suspicious. He was sitting just along from me here until a short while ago. Do you know who I mean?' I saw him nod and I continued. 'Do you think he might be our man?'

I had to wait a few seconds while he considered the question. Finally, he came to a conclusion. 'I don't think so. He's a wimpy sort of character and I can't see what reason he might have had to kill Beck. He barely talks to anybody and he certainly hasn't been involved with any of the female guests – or, indeed, any of the male ones either. We all get the impression he's a bit of a loner, and the girls think he's maybe a voyeur, but I think he's probably inoffensive enough.'

'And did I understand right that he's in one of the luxury chalets?'

'That's right, number one.'

'I was wondering about going around to talk to him now, or do you think it might be better to wait until the morning?'

'I'd give it until the morning. It's not as if you've got anything definite against him so I would suggest you leave him in peace for tonight.'

I nodded in agreement. 'Okay. By the way, I was wondering if there were any day guests here at the Retreat on Saturday night who might have had the opportunity to commit the murder?'

He shook his head. 'Off the top of my head, I think there were four or five that day, but they would all have left before the restaurant closed and, according to the police, Beck was still alive then. I'll double-check but, no, the killer has to have been one of the people still here now.'

'What about Bianca Moretti? Was she here on Saturday?'

'I think so, but I'm not completely sure. Either way, she would have left early evening as she always had dinner with her father.'

'Might she have come back afterwards?'

'I think it's unlikely but I can check if you like. Each time a smart bracelet is used to open the pedestrian gate lock, it registers on the system, so we know everybody who's been in and out. I'll take a look but, like I say, it would have been unusual for her to have come back.' He caught my eye. 'Surely you can't think Bianca might have had anything to do with the death of Joe Beck? She could never do anything like that. I've known her for five years and she's as straight as a die.'

I didn't disabuse him. After all, she had served her time and deserved a second chance.

After George had left me, I drank the last of my now cold coffee and glanced down at Oscar. 'Feel like a walk?'

He did.

When I got back to my locker to put my clothes on again, the first thing I did was to check my phone to see if Anna had called. She hadn't, but there was a text from her. It was short and not particularly sweet.

I've got your message. We need to talk when you get back to Florence.

She was right, we did need to talk, but the terse tone of her message was chilling. I wondered about giving her a call but, as it was almost eleven o'clock by this time, I decided to wait until the morning.

9

THURSDAY VERY EARLY MORNING

I was woken early after a comfortable night's sleep marred only by thoughts of Anna. I was roused by the sound of banging on my door and Leo's voice.

'Dan, wake up, there's been another death at the Retreat.'

In a second, I was wide awake and I leapt out of bed, to the surprise of Oscar, who was still stretched out on the floor alongside me. I hurried over to the door and opened it to find Leo, dressed only in a pair of flowery blue and white Bermuda shorts, standing on the landing looking confused and concerned.

'Dan, it's happened again.'

'Leo, when you say there's been a death, do you mean a *suspicious* death?' Although this came as a shock, it wasn't altogether unwelcome. At least now I might have something more concrete to work with and the police would almost certainly have to rethink the decision they had made about Beck's death being a simple accident.

He nodded and held out his phone to show me a text message. Its content was brief and to the point.

I've just had a call from Berto. There's a body lying face down in the pool. I've called the police and I'm going down there now. G

I handed him back his phone. 'When did this message come in?'

'A minute ago, maybe two. The time it took me to pull on a pair of shorts.'

'I presume the message is from George, the manager. Who's Berto?'

'Alberto Romano, the guy who cuts the grass and skims the pool.'

'But we don't know the identity of the body yet?' He shook his head as I glanced at my empty wrist. 'What time is it?'

'Six thirty-five. In the summer, Berto starts at six-thirty.'

'Give me a couple of minutes to get dressed and I'll go down there.'

He nodded. 'I'm coming with you.'

Five minutes later, I was digging around in the van for Oscar's lead. I don't use it very often but as we were about to enter what might prove to be a murder scene, I was taking no chances. While I did this, Oscar had his early-morning pee against the umbrella pine and then returned to my side with a large pine cone in his mouth. He deposited it at my feet and gave me a hopeful look, but I had to disappoint him.

'Sorry dog, but there's no time to play fetch right now.'

I heard the door behind me slam and Leo appeared, now wearing a polo shirt. I clipped on the lead and the three of us hurried along to the main entrance of the Retreat. The barrier was down and the gatekeeper's cabin still locked. We went in through the steel gate and I was heading for the changing room when Leo grabbed my arm and shook his head. 'No time for that now, Dan. This is an emergency; keep your clothes on. Let's just get down to the pool.'

It was relatively crisp and fresh at this time of the morning and the sun was only just beginning to break through the early-morning haze on the hilltops. Under other circumstances, it would have been delightful, although today it was anything but.

When we got to the pool, I could see a man in blue overalls standing in the water up to his waist over on the far side, tugging a floating body towards the side. I immediately called across to him in Italian.

'Leave the body alone. I'm coming over.'

The man shot us a questioning look, but Leo gave him a reassuring nod and a wave in return and the man released his hold and made his way over to the steps as the body floated gently towards the side. We were hurrying around to join him when I heard the unmistakable sound of emergency service vehicles coming up the road to the camp. I stopped as I reached the edge of the pool where the body was floating and I crouched down to check for signs of life. A touch of the carotid artery on his neck confirmed that he was dead and from the stiffness of the body, I felt sure he had been dead for some hours.

From close up, it was clear it was a man and I couldn't miss the blue bruise and broken skin on the back of his neck. This looked like a carbon copy of Beck's murder. If it had been an accident, the chances of two such deaths in short succession in the same place with the same wounds were probably worse than of winning the lottery. Assuming it was murder, did this mean it had been carried out by the same perpetrator or was it maybe a copycat killing for whatever reason? I was turning over in my head the people I'd seen the previous day, wondering which of them this might be, when I heard running feet. A pair of uniformed police officers came down the path towards us, closely followed by a pair of paramedics.

While I stood to one side, the two officers – a man and a woman – started questioning Leo and a soaking-wet Berto about when and how the body had been discovered. Less than a minute later, George appeared, accompanied by a plain-clothes officer who immediately gave orders to secure the area and keep curious onlookers out of the way.

George pointed to Leo and introduced him. 'This is Inspector Luca Sartori. Luca, this is my boss, Leo Moretti; he owns the Retreat. I was at school with Luca and he's married to my cousin.'

They shook hands and I was impressed by the inspector's businesslike manner. Clearly, this wasn't the first time he had seen a dead body. I stood back while he shot off a number of questions and instructed his two officers to help the paramedics haul the body out of the water. I didn't want to interfere in his case so, while waiting to be introduced, I checked my phone for the first time since the previous night and was delighted to see an email from Paul at Scotland Yard. Its content was fascinating.

Hi Dan. Your man Joseph Beck is an interesting one. The passport is genuine but his name came up on the system. Interestingly, his file's been flagged, 'Authorised Access Only'. From the code alongside it, it looks like he was MI6. You used to have a friend over at Vauxhall Cross, didn't you, so maybe if you have a word with him? I'll keep digging and if I get anything more, I'll send it across. Good luck. P

Suddenly, the whole case took on a completely different complexion. It sounded as though the first victim might well have been a spy – or at least a member of some branch of the UK's security services – so had he been killed because of this, possibly by an assassin from a foreign power? Certainly here at the

Retreat, there were guests of eleven different nationalities so could it be...? But if that was the case, then did this signify that the latest body in the pool had also been a spy? As for my 'friend' at MI6 headquarters at Vauxhall Cross on the banks of the Thames, I had recently heard that he'd been promoted to a very senior position, so whether he would still remember the humble police inspector who had helped him out ten years earlier when his son had got into trouble with drugs was another matter. Still, I could but try.

My musings were interrupted by the sound of my name as Leo introduced me.

'This is Dan Armstrong. He's a private investigator. Dan, this is Inspector Sartori.'

I held out my hand and wasn't surprised to see an expression of suspicion appear on the face of the detective. He looked to me as if he was barely forty, which is pretty young for an inspector, and I hoped this meant he was good at his job. His suspicious expression was something to which I could easily relate. Back in my days as a police officer, I had resented intrusion into my investigations by third parties, particularly from people outside the force, and private eyes had been considered the lowest of the low. No doubt he saw me as, at best, a nuisance and, at worst, as a positive hindrance. I was about to explain my involvement in the case when the paramedics finally managed to drag the dripping corpse out of the water and turned it over.

There could be no doubt about it. Even without his trademark dark glasses, this was none other than Owen Griffiths, the man described as a creepy voyeur. I exchanged glances with George, who was looking as white as the corpse itself, but dead bodies can do that to people. Seeing that he needed a moment, I spoke to the inspector myself.

'The man's name is Griffiths, Owen Griffiths, and he's... he was British.'

The inspector gave me a curt nod of the head. 'Thank you, but can I ask what your involvement is?'

I didn't want to drop Leo in it by revealing that he'd called me in because he'd felt that the investigation into Beck's death had been unsatisfactory, so I produced something that was perfectly true, even if I did leave out a few minor details, like the fact that I was being paid for my time.

'I'm staying with Mr Moretti at the tower. I've known his daughter for a few years and she told me about this place. It sounded like an interesting and different sort of holiday so I came along to take a look.'

The inspector looked somewhat mollified and Leo shot me a surreptitious wink. I knew that the information I had just received from London would be of interest to the police as far as the first murder was concerned – and quite possibly this one as well – but I was loathe to reveal classified information to all and sundry so I decided to tread carefully.

'Inspector, could I have a word with you in private?'

He looked taken aback but he agreed, and the two of us walked along the poolside until we reached the far end, out of range of even Oscar's bionic hearing.

'I don't want you to think I'm trying to interfere, but yesterday, after people had told me about the death of Joseph Beck on Saturday night, I mentioned it to a friend of mine who's an inspector at Scotland Yard in London. He's just sent me an email which may well be of interest to you.' I pulled out my phone. 'How's your English? MI6 means the security services, in case the name's unfamiliar to you. Would you like me to translate?'

'I find myself using English more and more these days. It's not great, but I should be okay.' He was still sounding suspicious but I didn't blame him. I handed him the phone and watched as he read the text. He gave the phone back to me after a few moments and stood there, clearly studying me closely. Finally, he spoke. This time, his tone was more curious than suspicious.

'How is it that an inspector in the British police gives you this sort of highly sensitive information? Who exactly are you? Are you in the security services as well?'

'No, I've never been involved in that sort of thing, but I recently retired after thirty years in the Metropolitan Police murder squad. I was a detective chief inspector and Paul Wilson was one of my colleagues and he's remained a good friend. Now that I've set up my own private investigation bureau, I sometimes turn to him for help if a case has UK links.'

I saw him digest this information and he nodded a couple of times. 'As you say, this information *is* potentially significant. When we looked into the death here last Saturday night, there was nothing to suggest foul play, but this could potentially change everything.' He looked up, caught my eye and gave a reluctant shrug of the shoulders. 'This new evidence means I'll have to reopen that case.'

I could sympathise with his position. Having to go back on a decision can be tough – especially if your superiors pick up on it. I gave him a little smile. 'If it helps, you can blame anything you like on me. Besides, this is brand-new evidence that you didn't have access to at the weekend.'

I was impressed to see him produce an answering smile. 'Thanks, I'll bear that in mind. And thanks for letting me know this.' I saw his eyes flick down the pool to where the two uniformed officers had very sensibly led Leo, Berto and George away and the paramedics had covered the body of Owen Griffiths with a sheet. 'The body of the first victim was found in almost identical circumstances. Did you know that?'

'Yes, that's what people here have been telling me. Right down to the bruising on the back of the neck. I've just been wondering whether both deaths might be the work of the same perpetrator. If not, it's either a hell of a coincidence or somebody's deliberately trying to make it look as if the same person did both. There's something else you need to know that might prove significant.' I went on to relate to him what Sophie had told me the previous evening about Owen Griffiths claiming to have known that the first death had been murder. When I got to the end of my account, I shook my head sadly. 'I should have questioned him last night but I decided to wait. The guy had gone off to bed and I didn't want to disturb him.'

'Don't worry about it. It's not as if you were the investigating officer, after all. I wonder why he said that and why he didn't say anything last weekend. It could be that he heard or saw something more recently and that's what he meant when he spoke to the waitress last night. Maybe the murderer overheard what he said and decided to silence him before he could say any more. Did she say if there was anybody else around when he told her?'

'No, and I didn't ask. Sorry, I should have done, but I imagine she'll be here pretty soon if she isn't already. By the way, you do realise this is a naturist camp? It came as a considerable surprise to me yesterday.'

He grinned. 'You never know, it might make this case a bit more interesting. Now, I'd better get onto the nuts and bolts of working out exactly who was here last night and if anybody saw or heard anything. I might as well start with you. Your name's Dan Armstrong and you said you had dinner here last night; when did you go back to the tower?'

'Just after half past ten, probably no more than fifteen or twenty minutes after the victim went off to his chalet, and, as far as I could tell, most people had already gone to bed. By the way, I understand that this whole area around the swimming pool is illuminated until 11 p.m. so the killer – if indeed this really was murder – probably waited until after that to commit the crime. It'll be interesting to hear what the pathologist thinks as far as time of death's concerned, but I know that with bodies immersed in water, it's notoriously difficult to be precise.'

He nodded in agreement. 'Yes indeed, and thanks for that information.' He held out his hand to me again. 'I appreciate your cooperation and, please, if you can think of anything else that might advance the investigation, just let me know. I'll be very grateful.' He handed me one of his cards and I gave him one of mine in return, thankful that this time, I had actually been able to bring my phone and wallet with me. He glanced at my card and looked up. 'You're based in Florence? That's why you speak such good Italian. It's a beautiful city.'

'It certainly is, but in the summer it just gets so packed with tourists, it's hard to breathe. I was in San Clemente Spiaggia yesterday and there were quite a few people around, but nothing like as many as in Florence.'

'Just wait two weeks; that's when it all kicks off here. Suddenly, the whole place will be invaded by screaming kids and lonely wives who've been dumped down here by their husbands while *they* go back to their offices in Milan and Turin to wine and dine their secretaries. With so many people around, the crime rate here shoots right up from mid-June until mid-September.'

'You mentioned using your English quite a lot; does that mean there are lots of British tourists here?'

He shook his head. 'There are some, of course, but the majority of the English speakers are Americans. The big cruise ships moor up in Genoa or across the border on the Côte d'Azur and they bring them into places like Alassio and San Clemente by the trainload. It's also an area that's very popular with

Germans and other nationalities, so very often the lingua franca is English.'

'Well, if you need any help with interpreting or translating, just give me a call. I'll be here all day today. I'm supposed to be going back to Florence tomorrow night but I could maybe stay if you need me.' I felt I had to make the offer although I had told Anna I would be back the following night and I was already in a deep hole as far as relations with her were concerned so I hoped I wouldn't be asked to stay on.

'Thanks. At this stage, it's hard to say what help I'll need but do feel free to nose around as much as you like and if you find out anything, I'll be very happy to hear about it.'

10

THURSDAY EARLY MORNING

Leo and I went back to the tower a bit later on for a shower and breakfast and we discussed what had happened over bacon and eggs, accompanied by strong coffee from his all-singing, all-dancing coffee machine. He was looking troubled and I could well imagine what was going through his mind so I said it for him.

'It looks like you were right, Leo. Beck and Griffiths were both murdered, there's no other explanation; *two* accidents or suicides in the exact same manner would be just too incredible for words. What we've got to work out now is why they were killed and to what extent, if any, the two deaths are linked. Once we've sorted that out, hopefully we'll have a clearer idea of who did it. Any ideas?'

Leo was clearly thinking hard. 'The only common denominator is that they were both British but otherwise, they seem to have had little or nothing in common. All I can assume is that Griffiths was killed by the same person who killed Beck in order to silence him. I wonder if Griffiths really knew something, or if he was just shooting his mouth off. Do we think he saw something on Saturday night?'

I nodded. I had passed on Sophie's snippet of information to Leo, but I made no mention of the message from Scotland Yard about Beck's possible link to the security services. That was definitely not in the public domain. 'That seems the most likely explanation, but why didn't he say something at the time? If only I'd managed to speak to him last night.' I gave a frustrated snort but Leo was quick to reassure me.

'Who knows? If you had done, *you* might be floating in the pool alongside him.'

I hadn't considered this. 'You might be right, Leo. We'll never know, will we? Inspector Sartori wondered if it was maybe something Griffiths saw or heard more recently.'

Leo gave me an interrogative look. 'More recently? Did he mean Griffiths heard the murderer talking about Joe Beck's killing?'

'Yes, or maybe he saw him disposing of the murder weapon or he stumbled on a significant clue. By the way, I'm talking as if the murderer was a man but there's no reason why a reasonably fit woman couldn't have done it. Mind you, it's pretty clear the murders must have taken place down at the pool, otherwise trying to carry the unconscious body of a big man like Griffiths would be more than most people could manage – male or female. Of course, if Griffiths overheard the murderer talking, then that would mean that there has to be another person at the Retreat who was in on the killing as well. I must admit, I've been tending to concentrate my attention on people travelling alone up till now but, thinking about it, a couple would be less conspicuous and would explain how Griffiths might have overheard talk.'

'That makes a lot of sense, but the question is who?'

Who indeed? After a brief silence, I changed the subject to somebody closer to home; I still had a feeling that Bianca and her father knew more about this than they had told me.

'Did Bianca have dinner with you last Saturday?' He nodded so I continued. 'Might she have gone back over to the Retreat afterwards? Maybe to see a friend?'

He shook his head. 'No, she was here with me all night.' He looked up sharply. 'You're not seriously considering her as a suspect?'

'Of course not, it's just that I'm trying to establish who was where that night and last night in case they might have seen something.' I shot him a reassuring grin. 'As far as last night's concerned, you have me as an alibi and I have you, so we should be beyond suspicion. Now, let's see if we can identify any suspicious couples.'

I pulled out the printout that Leo had given me with the names of the different guests, but there were so many couples, it was hard to know where to start. Making up my mind, I stood up.

'It's no good, Leo; there's nothing much I can do from the sidelines. I'm going to go back to the Retreat and if the inspector's there. I'll tell him I'd like to join in, even if it's just to help with interpreting. He sounded very approachable and he even thanked me for passing on what I heard last night. If only I could get my eyes on their report on Beck's death and if only I could find out more about Griffiths. First things first, I'm going to try my friend at Scotland Yard again and see if he'd mind doing a bit of digging about the latest victim.'

I decided to call Paul rather than text him as I knew I was imposing on him with all these requests. He sounded pleased to hear from me and was quick to assure me that I wasn't putting him to any trouble – although I knew I was.

'Don't worry about it, Dan. God knows, you've helped me enough. Let me have Griffiths' passport number and I'll take it from there. It shouldn't take long to find out if he's on the police system or if he's clean, and just exactly who he was and what he did for a job. I'll get back to you ASAP but, in the meantime, I was going to send you a message anyway to give you a little snippet of information. You're not the only one with friends in the security services. I had a word with somebody who works over there – just in admin – and she told me that Beck had a reputation as a womaniser. "A right little James Bond" were her exact words.'

'That certainly ties in with what I've heard about him here. Do you happen to know if he was married? Might there be a jealous wife or partner in the background?'

'I asked, but she didn't know. Like I say, she's not at the sharp end and if he was an active agent, all that stuff would be a closely guarded secret.'

I thanked him for his help and wondered whether I should try dialling the highly confidential personal number of Graham Oldman-Davis, now among the most powerful figures at MI6 and generally referred to by most of his underlings by his initials, G-O-D: 'God'. In the end, I decided not to disturb the great man unless it was absolutely necessary. Maybe when I spoke to Inspector Sartori, he might already have come up with some amazing new evidence that would crack the case without me needing to contact the spymaster.

Dragging a reluctant Oscar away from the smell of bacon – needless to say, he had disposed of the rinds – I went back to the Retreat. I stopped at the gate for a few moments, wondering whether to carry on fully clothed or whether to strip off again. In the end, I decided to leave my clothes in the locker so that, as far as the other guests at the Retreat were concerned, it wouldn't look too much as though I was involved with the investigation. This time, I had a bright idea and, after discarding my clothes, I used the plastic bag that had contained my new flip-flops to carry my wallet, notepad and phone. I started by walking down to the swimming pool to see if the inspector was there. He wasn't, but I recognised the female officer who had been one of the first on the scene. Behind her, four officers in disposable overalls were at work and a masked figure that looked to me like the pathologist was crouching down, carefully studying the body.

As I approached the officer, she must have recognised me because she gave me a salute – presumably, the inspector had told her who I was – and then I saw her cheeks flush bright red and I suddenly realised that, while she and the other officers were all fully clothed, I was of course now completely naked. Sophie was right: I really had forgotten. Needless to say, seeing the officer looking embarrassed made me feel embarrassed as well and I felt my own cheeks begin to colour, but shielded myself as best I could with my bag and did my best to sound blasé.

'Sorry, Officer, but I've got into the habit of dressing, or rather undressing, like the other guests here so as to blend in. Why don't you concentrate your attention on Oscar?'

Hearing his name, Oscar took the hint and wandered over to her side. As a result, she bent down and stroked his head while I queried where the inspector was. Without raising her eyes, she pointed vaguely in the direction of the bar/restaurant.

'He's questioning people at the bar, sir.'

'Is that the pathologist over there by the water?'

Still directing all her attention at my dog, she nodded. 'Yes, sir.'

'And is that the same pathologist who attended the Saturday night murder?' She shook her head and I decided to see to what extent the inspector had accepted me. The constable calling me 'sir' was definitely a good sign. 'Do you think it might be possible for me to have a word with this pathologist?'

'Yes, sir, I'm sure it would. The inspector said you were helping with the investigation.'

This definitely sounded very positive so I asked her if she would mind looking after Oscar, who by now was stretched out on his back on the stone slabs while she scratched his tummy. She nodded – still without looking up at me – so I asked her to hold his lead and went over to the body.

When I got there, the pathologist looked up and, at the exact same moment that I realised she was female, she realised that the man standing above her was naked. Full marks to her, however, she didn't bat an eyelid.

'Good morning. I'd be grateful if you'd keep that thing out of my face. In my experience, they're unpredictable and can be dangerous.' No prizes for guessing what she was referring to. With the overalls, mask and headscarf, it was hard to see much of her, but I definitely got the impression that her eyes were smiling. I took a hasty step back, clasping my plastic bag in front of me, and gave her a smile in return.

'Sorry to appear like this but I'm trying to blend in. I don't know if Inspector Sartori's told you, my name's Dan Armstrong and I'm—'

'The hotshot detective from England. Yes, he did mention you, but he didn't mention your choice of uniform. Is that how all police officers in England are dressed?'

'No, it's far too cold and wet for that. Can I ask if you've found anything interesting?'

'A couple of things: as I'm sure you've seen for yourself, it's almost exactly the same modus operandi as the previous death.

He received a blow to the back of the head and then he fell or was pushed into the water, and I wouldn't mind betting I'll find a high alcohol level in his blood like last time. I didn't do the post-mortem on the previous victim. That was my colleague and, as he had found bloodstains and some of the victim's hair on the edge of one of the poolside slabs, he logically assumed this had rendered the victim unconscious and that it had been an unfortunate accident. Now that this has happened, I'm looking on it in a different light.'

She rose to her feet and I felt relief that her eyes were now level with my chest. 'We haven't released the body of the first victim yet so I'll do a full autopsy on both bodies when I get back, because I've spotted something interesting on this one. Although we've located a spot a bit further along the edge of the pool with what appears to be vestiges of blood, tissue and hair, I can see quite clearly even from here that the victim was struck twice, once by a rough edge – presumably against one of the poolside slabs – but he was also struck very forcibly by a rounded weapon, like a wooden club or iron bar that cracked his skull and would have rendered him unconscious. When I get him back to the lab, I should be able to give a clearer idea of the size and shape of the weapon.'

I nodded slowly. 'So presumably the victim was knocked out by the first blow, made with something smooth and round, and then the murderer deliberately banged the man's head against the stone slab to produce the illusion of an accident.'

'Precisely, and somehow I have a feeling I'm going to find the same thing happened to the first body, too.'

'So your gut feeling is that we have two murders on our hands and no question of anything accidental?'

'No doubt at all about this one and I imagine the same will turn out to be the case with the first. We've also located some minute drops of blood a bit further away from the edge of the pool, over by that bench, and I wouldn't mind betting that we'll find they match with the victim's. Somebody assaulted him over there and then tried to make it look like an accident.'

'If there's blood on the ground, would the murderer's clothes have been spattered as well?' No sooner had I spoken than I realised my mistake. 'What am I saying? Almost certainly the killer wasn't wearing clothes so a quick dip in the pool or a shower and all traces are gone.'

'Exactly.'

She pulled off her mask and headscarf and I saw from her greying hair that she was probably three or four years older than I was. She gave me another little smile. 'Are pathologists well paid in England?'

'I have no idea, but I wouldn't mind betting that they're paid better than police officers. Why, are you thinking of a move?'

'No, just curious. So what's the deal with you, then? Are you here in an official capacity or did this all come as a big surprise to you?'

'A little bit of both. I left the police a couple of years ago and it's good to keep my hand in.'

She glanced around to check that we weren't being overheard. 'I was at a wedding at the weekend – my daughter's – and I'm sorry my locum didn't pick up anything suspicious as far as Saturday night's victim was concerned.' I saw her eyes scour the surroundings. 'Are you going to see the inspector now?'

'Yes, apparently he's conducting interviews up at the restaurant.'

'Then would you tell him that, if he's happy to release the body to my people now, I'll do my best to get my report to him by mid-afternoon?'

'Of course. Thanks for filling me in. I would shake your hand, but...'

Collecting Oscar from the police constable – who studiously kept her eyes trained on her shoes throughout the process – I headed away from the pool in the direction of the clubhouse. I checked the time and saw that it was almost eight o'clock and a little crowd had gathered at the bar. Over to one side, I could see the inspector sitting at a table with a different uniformed officer, and it looked as though they were going through their notes together. I decided to leave them to it for now and headed over to the bar to order an espresso. The conversation around me was mostly in German but I heard a couple of Italian voices and took my coffee over towards them in an attempt to engage them in conversation. They were quite a young couple, maybe in their late twenties or early thirties, and they looked up as Oscar and I approached. I decided to plead ignorance.

'What's going on? There are police officers everywhere.'

The man was quick to reply. 'There's been another fatality. A body's been found down at the pool.'

'Really?' I've always been pretty good at sounding gormless. 'Was it another accident? Like Saturday?'

This time, it was the woman who answered, her tone highly sceptical. 'Some accident! They were both murdered. We've said it all along, haven't we, Vincenzo?'

He nodded. 'There's no way the first guy could have drowned. My wife and I've seen him swimming. He swam like a professional. No, he was murdered all right, and now the killer's struck again and they're saying this latest victim's another Englishman.'

Whether Owen Griffiths from Wales would have approved of being called English was a moot point but, sadly for him, it was unlikely to bother him now. Still sounding clueless, I tried to find out if they knew anything more.

'But murder? What can either of the victims have done to make somebody want to kill them?'

There was fear in the wife's voice as she replied. 'That's what we've just been saying. It sounds to me like it's some crazy, random killer, so that means we could be next. The police have taken our ID cards and passports and said we all have to stay here, otherwise we'd be packing up and leaving straight away.'

'Have you spoken to the police?'

The husband answered. 'No, but Giorgio says we're all going to be interviewed in the course of the day and we just have to stay put for now. It'll be all right, dear.' He patted his wife's arm and I could see he was doing his best to allay her fears so I decided to add a little bit of reassurance of my own.

'I used to be in the police in Britain and that's just standard practice, so don't worry. And with a heavy police presence, you'll be quite safe if there is a killer on the rampage although, in my experience, most murders are for a specific reason.'

'But what could the reason be?' The husband sounded puzzled. 'Why them?'

'And not us?' His wife still wasn't reassured but there was little more I could say so I glanced over at the inspector's table.

'Seeing as there's a British connection, I think I'll go and ask if the police need any help with interpreting. Don't worry, I'm sure it'll all be sorted out soon.'

After draining the last of my coffee and setting the cup down on the bar, I walked across to the table where Inspector Sartori was sitting. He looked up as he saw me, suppressed a grin, and beckoned to me. 'Come and join us. I'm beginning to feel a bit overdressed.' He glanced across at his companion and made the introductions. 'Rossi, this is Chief Inspector Armstrong of the London murder squad.'

'*Formerly* of the murder squad. I'm in the private sector nowadays.' I held out my hand to the officer beside him and, spotting the stripes on his shoulders, I addressed him with his rank. 'I'm pleased to meet you, Sergeant Rossi.'

He was probably twenty years older than the inspector, pretty close to my age, and he had the look of an experienced career police officer. He gave me a little grin as we shook hands.

'I see you're blending in. I've seen more naked bodies this morning than in all my years in the police force put together.'

I grinned back. 'It saves a lot of time on pressing your trousers and it's unexpectedly liberating.'

Returning my attention to the inspector, I passed on the pathologist's message and he immediately instructed Sergeant Rossi to go and give the order to release the body. After the sergeant had gone off, Sartori waved me into the vacant seat.

'Have you come up with anything fresh?'

'Have you heard what the pathologist says about two blows to the victim's head?' I saw him nod and I continued. 'She says that confirms the idea that Griffiths was murdered. I've asked my friend at the Metropolitan Police to look into the background of this latest victim and he told me that the first victim had a reputation as a womaniser.' I used the Italian word, *donnaiolo*, which has the same pejorative overtones.

Inspector Sartori nodded a couple of times. 'I've just been talking to Giorgio and he said the same thing – although he couldn't say whether Beck hooked up with any particular woman here.' A smile appeared on his face. 'Before I forget, I have a message for you. It's from a friend of yours and he said, "Tell Dan to make sure he doesn't catch cold without his knickers on."'

I smiled back. 'Wise words. And who was that?'

'Inspector Virgilio Pisano of the Florence murder squad.' Seeing the surprise on my face, he explained. 'I'm afraid I have a suspicious nature and when I saw that you were based in

Florence, I made a call to a friend of mine who works at the *questura* there to ask if they knew you. They put me through to Inspector Pisano, who speaks of you in glowing terms.'

'Virgilio's one of my very best friends. He's helped me out a lot and it was he who suggested I set up my own investigation agency. I've helped him a few times with cases involving English speakers and we work well together. In fact, his wife now works for me. As for you having a suspicious nature, I'm delighted to hear it. In your position, I would almost certainly have done the same thing. A very sensible precaution. Anyway, like I said, if there's any help I can give, just ask.'

Sartori looked only too pleased at my offer. 'My plan is to do a brief interview with all the staff members first and then, later this morning, to start interviewing the guests. According to Giorgio, although the majority of people here are northern Europeans, they almost all speak some English so we should be able to conduct the interviews in that language rather than hunting around for interpreters who speak Swedish or German or Dutch. You mentioned you'd be happy to help out with interpreting and I'd be very grateful if you could. It would also be a great help to me to have an officer of your experience alongside me, so if anything occurs to you and you want to ask any questions of your own, please do. Just make sure you rattle off a quick translation into Italian so that Rossi can take it all down.'

'I'll be happy to help, Inspector. What time do you want me?'

He looked at his watch. 'It's almost eight-thirty and I shouldn't think interviewing the staff will take more than an hour or so. How about if we say ten o'clock?'

'That's fine. In that case, I think I'll go and take my dog for a good long walk first. Where are you going to do the interviews?'

'Giorgio says I can use his office in the clubhouse.'

That sounded good. 'In that case, I won't bother stripping off when I come back. That way, you and Rossi won't have to put up with having a naked man alongside you all the time. And, from my point of view, that means I'll have pockets. Naturism may well have its appeal but it does make carrying stuff tricky. I'm beginning to understand why women carry handbags.'

11

THURSDAY MORNING

I left the inspector at his table and went back to the changing room where I sat down and spent a few minutes scribbling down names of people and facts I had learned so far this morning. Once I had written down all I could recall, I pulled on my clothes and Oscar and I walked out onto the open hillside, where we followed a rough track that led inland, away from the sea.

The sky was clear and it would no doubt turn out to be another scorching-hot day but, for now, the temperature was refreshingly cool. As we walked, it became clear that the Retreat and the tower were at the end of a long promontory that extended from here all the way back up into the tree-covered hills behind the coast. These were the Ligurian Apennines that protect the Italian Riviera from the worst of the winter weather coming down from the north, giving it a generally mild microclimate similar to that of the Côte d'Azur. Little wonder that wealthy Brits chose to come here in the nineteenth century to get away from the air pollution of industrial Britain and the ever-present risk of lung disease.

The air was certainly clean up here, but the terrain was rough with rocky outcrops. Little was growing apart from scrub, wild thyme and rosemary. There was a strong aroma of herbs in the air but I've never been great at horticulture so I could only name a few of them. Gorse and broom bushes covered in yellow flowers dotted the landscape along with occasional stunted thorn trees, from whose branches the twittering of little birds reinforced how untouched it was up here. Lizards darted away as we passed and I hoped there were none of their legless cousins around. I've never liked snakes.

As I walked, I kept turning over in my head what had happened and kept asking myself what possible connection there might be between the two deaths. I was still thinking about this almost an hour later when we returned to the camp once more, this time on a narrow path that skirted close to the perimeter of the wire fence. It was as we were only twenty or thirty yards from the fence that I spotted something. Oscar, as usual, had been bringing me sticks to throw for him to retrieve and I was just launching a gnarly bit of wood along the path for him when my attention was attracted by something glistening in the under-growth. Out of curiosity, I stopped and peered through the branches of a wild rosemary bush and found myself confronted by a gleaming steel bar, just over a foot long, part embedded in the sandy soil where it had landed nose first. Because of its pristine condition, it obviously hadn't been out here exposed to the elements for long, and bells immediately began ringing in my head.

I looked back over my shoulder and did a bit of dead reckoning. As far as I could see, we were only a stone's throw – or in this case a steel bar's throw – from the corner of the swimming pool complex, although that was well hidden behind the wire fence and the thick hedge. Unless I was very much mistaken, what I was looking at might well turn out to be the murder weapon – or at least one of them – lobbed over the fence by the killer either on Saturday night or the previous night to get rid of it.

I still had my plastic bag of valuables stuffed in my pocket so I quickly removed phone, notepad and wallet so as to free it up. After taking a couple of photos to show the location of the weapon and the way it had ended up almost upright in the ground, I carefully picked it up and slipped it into the bag without touching it with my bare hands. It was very solid and very heavy and it didn't take me long to work out what it was. I had seen this sort of thing before and, indeed, in my regular visits to the gym over the years, I'd often used one. Both ends had a screw thread and this had to be what's known in the world of weight training as a hand dumbbell bar. Just like the long bars with massive weights at either end that weightlifters use in the Olympics, these shorter bars are specifically designed to carry weights for single arm and forearm strengthening. I had a feeling that if I were to visit Rita in the Retreat gym, she would be surprised to discover that she was missing one. Of course, if she had committed the murder herself, she wouldn't be surprised at all.

I returned to the camp, this time not stopping to disrobe, and saw the sergeant, accompanied by Freddie, just disappearing into the clubhouse. She was recognisable even from behind by her pink hair. I didn't want to disturb the interview so I took a seat in the same place as the previous evening. I was impressed to see that all the people around me were still naked. Clearly the fact that they were about to be interviewed by the police wasn't going to change their naturist instincts. The four old men were playing cards again and the four wives were deep in discussion about something on a different table. Almost a dozen tables were occupied and there was a palpable air of concern around the place. A few moments after I had sat down, Sophie appeared. She also had a worried expression on her face, which softened a bit when she spotted Oscar. She bent down to ruffle his ears and glanced sideways at me.

'George says you're helping the police. Have they said anything about who they think did it?' I saw her eyes land on the plastic bag on the table in front of me but she didn't ask what was in it and I didn't offer to tell her. I just shook my head for now.

'I'm waiting to speak to the inspector now. Maybe he knows something, but at the moment, it's still early stages. He said his plan is to start interviewing everybody this morning and I'm supposed to help him with translating. Has he spoken to you?'

'Yes, and I told him what I told you last night.'

'Did you tell him who was near you when Griffiths spoke to you?'

'Yes, I tried to, but the place was busy at the time and I can't really remember terribly well. Griffiths was sitting at his usual table and I know the Duponts had just arrived alongside him, and I'm pretty sure one of the tables in front of him was occupied by Mr Smith and his girlfriend, but I can't for the life of me remember who was on the next table along, or the one on the other side of him. I seem to think there were couples on both, but that's as far as it goes.'

I did my best to sound encouraging. 'Don't worry, it'll probably come back to you at three o'clock in the morning.'

'Can I get you something to drink? A glass of brandy maybe? That's what I feel like.'

Considering it was ten o'clock in the morning, I felt that was pushing it a bit. 'I think I'll just have an espresso and a glass of cold water, please.'

She went off to get my drinks and I continued surveying the scene. There was no sign of Love and Peace Melinda, Kim the model or the grumpy poodle, but I did recognise a few of the other faces from my walkabout the previous day and one or two people even managed to give me a smile or a wave. I sent a voice message to Anna back in Florence – not about our relationship this time, but about the case. I'd been planning not to say anything for fear that she start worrying but, following the phone call from the inspector, Virgilio now knew all about it. He would no doubt tell Lina, who was good friends with Anna. It was only fair Anna should hear from me first. I finished the message by assuring her that it was all being handled by a very efficient police inspector and my involvement was going to be minimal. As I said those last words, I felt Oscar's nose nudge my knee and I looked down to see him looking sceptical. I sometimes wonder how much he understands so I tapped him gently on the nose.

'I just didn't want her to worry, Oscar. That's all.' To what extent she would have been worried remained the big unknown after Tuesday night's debacle at the medieval fair.

He dropped his head back on the floor again, only to jump to his feet almost immediately when Sophie returned with my drinks and another bowl of water for him. Just before she went off, I asked her a question. 'The British couple you mentioned, Mr Smith and his girlfriend: can you point them out to me if they're here?'

She glanced around and then pointed. I immediately recognised the pink-skinned couple I had noticed the previous day and took a closer look at them. Yesterday, I had definitely got the impression that there had been tension between them, and this morning, it was even more evident. The body language alone spoke volumes; the woman was probably in her late thirties or early forties, was slim and looked fit, but what struck me was the fact that she was visibly far from happy. She had positioned herself not only on the opposite side of the table from her boyfriend but she had tilted her chair away from him so that he was, in effect, looking at her left shoulder while she was staring out towards the pool. For his part, he was ostentatiously ignoring her and, indeed, every time another woman walked past, his eyes followed her without any attempt at dissimulation. Clearly, for whatever reason, these two weren't happy bunnies. Why? I wondered. Was this just domestic disharmony or might there be more to it than that?

'I believe there's another British couple here, a Mr and Mrs Harcourt. I don't suppose you can see them, can you?'

Sophie looked around and was just turning back towards me when she suddenly pointed down towards the path leading from the swimming pool. 'There they are, there.' She gave me a little grin. 'Freddie and I call her the duchess and him the general.'

Intrigued, I checked them out as they walked up the path towards the bar. They were probably around my age and they both looked fit. I could immediately see why they had got their nicknames. The woman's faded blonde hair had been piled up on her head in a most elegant manner and she looked for all the world as if she were just about to slip into a ballgown for a high-class soirée. She was even wearing pendant earrings, which looked singularly out of place considering she was otherwise naked. Her husband was a foot taller than her and he wasn't walking up the path; he was marching. It didn't need the perfectly trimmed moustache to confirm why the staff here had awarded him a military rank.

Did they look like a pair of murderers? No, but looks can be deceptive.

I had just finished my coffee when Freddie emerged from the clubhouse and I immediately picked up the plastic bag containing the steel bar and walked in. The female uniformed officer was standing by a door marked 'Manager' and I headed across to her, relieved for her sake that I was now fully clothed. Even so, her cheeks coloured a bit as she saw me.

'Does the inspector have anybody in there with him? I'd like a word, if possible.'

'The last interview just finished, so you can go on in by all means, sir.'

She opened the door for me, and Oscar and I went inside. Inspector Sartori looked up and beckoned me over to the desk where he was sitting, and I didn't waste any time. I went across to him and laid the plastic bag on the desktop.

'I found this out in the scrub, about twenty or thirty metres from the fence, not far from the pool complex. I have a feeling it might be one of the murder weapons.' I pulled out my phone and showed him photos of the steel bar sticking up out of the ground and its location.

The inspector opened the bag and peered inside and the sergeant came over to take a look as well as I continued. 'No bloodstains that I could see but, if we're lucky, there might be prints or even the killer's DNA.'

The inspector handed the bag to the sergeant. 'Rossi, get this to the lab as soon as possible and send somebody down to the gym area to see whether they're missing one or maybe two of these. If the answer is two, then organise a party to search around the perimeter within, say, fifty or sixty metres.' The sergeant took the bag and went out of the door and I heard him in conversation with the officer outside. In the meantime, Inspector Sartori waved me into a seat to one side of the desk, leaving a pair of chairs in front of him for interviewees. He gave me a smile as Oscar wandered over to be petted.

'Well done, Chief Inspector.' Although we were speaking Italian, he deliberately used my former title in English. 'Who knows? We might get lucky.'

'Any joy interviewing the members of staff? Anybody see anything, hear anything?'

He repeated what Sophie had told me about her uncertainty as to exactly who might have been within earshot of Griffiths' comment to her the previous night. He then went on to tell me that, although not all of the staff had watertight alibis for the period between 9 p.m. and midnight the previous night, he had been unable to find any possible motive any of them might have had for murdering Beck – apart from one couple.

I felt sure I knew who he meant. 'Rita from the gym or her husband?'

'Exactly, Rita and Dario Dolcedo. She refused to open up to me, but I could see that she was holding back, and it's pretty clear from what some of the others said that she and the first victim were close. The husband looked shocked when I asked if his wife had had any involvement with Beck and he denied it most strenuously. I must admit I tended to believe him, but whether that's just a reflection on his lack of awareness or whether there really was nothing going on between them remains unknown for the moment. Beck was here last year as well and it could be the relationship between him and Rita – if there was one – started then. I'll call her back in after we've spoken to all the guests. If that steel bar *is* the murder weapon, it's quite a coincidence that it comes from her place of work.'

I nodded but added a word of caution. 'Yes, but maybe too convenient, unless she's stupid.'

'I know what you mean but, in my experience, not all killers are criminal masterminds. She still might be our murderer. Anyway, as far as I'm concerned, at least for the moment I'm tending to exclude all the rest of the staff, with the exception of her husband, and I'm ever more convinced that the killer has to be one of the guests.'

I nodded again. 'That's pretty much the conclusion I've come to as well. Could any of them come up with suggestions as to the identity of the perpetrator? I gather that some of the guests come back year after year and are pretty well known here, so it might be worth paying special attention to any newcomers. It seems unlikely to me that the killer would be foolish enough to commit murder in a place where he or she was well known.'

'I agree.' He glanced down at his notepad. 'Over fifty potential suspects, eleven different nationalities. It's going to take a while. I've got my people contacting police forces in the different countries but, realistically, we probably aren't going to get too much in the way of detail until tomorrow.' He looked up at me. 'And the problem is that tomorrow's Friday and twenty of the current guests are due to leave on Saturday. We've collected all the ID cards and passports and I've given instructions that nobody's to leave without my permission, but without something concrete against any of them, I can't see that I'll be able to hold them any longer than that, so I really need to crack the case in the next twenty-four hours.' He gave me a wry smile. 'So no pressure...'

I sympathised and offered all the support I could. A minute later, the sergeant returned and the interviews started. We spent all of the rest of the morning slowly working our way through every single guest, asking the same questions to each of them. These were:

Where were you between nine and twelve last night and can anybody vouch for that?

Did you have any contact with either of the victims?

Did you see or hear anything suspicious?

Can you offer any suggestions as to who might have committed one or both murders?

The interviews, albeit brief, still kept us busy until a quarter past one and the inspector and I were both almost hoarse by that time. As the door finally closed on a red-faced – and bottomed – German gentleman from Hamburg, Sartori sat back and stretched his legs and at that moment, the female officer reappeared with some interesting news.

'The woman at the gym is missing two steel bars so we've been searching and the second one has been found, sir. It was about twenty metres outside the fence, lying in the scrub. We've sent it to the lab for analysis.'

'Thank you, Pellegrino.' The officer went off with a satisfied look on her face. It's always good to be the bearer of good news.

The inspector gave a little grunt of satisfaction. 'I don't think there's much doubt that these were the murder weapons, and it adds even more weight to the assumption that both murders were committed by the same perpetrator. Now all we've got to do is to work out who that was.' He glanced across at the sergeant. 'Who's your money on, Rossi?'

The sergeant consulted his notes. 'There's the gym instructor herself and her husband, if he was aware of what's alleged to have been going on between her and the first victim, but otherwise nobody else on the staff who stands out. As far as the campers are concerned, I make it twenty-six of the people we've just seen have solid alibis, not just provided by their partners. A lot of the older Germans were playing cards and there was some sort of party in the two French campervans. Of the rest, I think the model and her roommate, the Mullers from Germany, the Czech and the German who were travelling alone all warrant further investigation.'

The inspector turned to me. 'Chief Inspector?'

'Just call me Dan. Everybody does.' I glanced at the sergeant. 'And the same applies to you, Sergeant. I fully agree with your choices – Mr Muller in particular looked very nervous about something – and I think I would add the two English couples.

Sophie the waitress said Jeremy Smith and his girlfriend were sitting close by when Owen Griffiths said that thing to her about it definitely being murder and the man struck me as a bit too cocky. They're clearly uptight about something and I'd like to know what the cause might be. The girlfriend's a good-looking woman, the same sort of age as the first victim, so maybe there's a story there. As for Mr and Mrs Harcourt, maybe it's just because both victims were British and they're British, but there was something about them that didn't ring true.' I turned the question back on the inspector. 'What about you? Anybody to add to the list?'

He glanced down at his notes. 'I wasn't convinced that the Hungarian couple were telling the whole truth: Laszlo and Maria Farkas from Budapest. You must remember them: the blonde with the tattoos and the husband built like Schwarzenegger? I make that a total of fourteen potential suspects but none that really stick out a mile.' He got to his feet and looked across at me. 'Feeling hungry? The least I can do is to buy you a good meal.'

'No need for that, I've enjoyed being back in harness again.'

And I had. I also realised with a start that I hadn't thought about Anna once since early morning. The main reason my ex-wife divorced me was that she had felt that in our relationship, she had always come second to my job. Was history about to repeat itself?

12

THURSDAY AFTERNOON

We had lunch at the Retreat and it was predictably excellent. As a starter, I opted for soft burrata cheese on a bed of cold roast aubergines, laced with fresh pesto. I followed this with *vitello tonnato* and salad. This dish consisted of thin slices of cold veal smothered in a creamy sauce made with mayonnaise, tuna and capers, and the salad was a delicious mix of iceberg lettuce and rocket leaves, sprinkled with slivers of parmesan and doused in extra virgin olive oil. I was pleasantly surprised when Sophie brought out the half-empty bottle of Pigato wine left over from last night, which they had meticulously recorked, labelled with my name, and kept in the fridge overnight. The two police officers looked pleased to hear that I was a fan of their local white and the inspector insisted on getting a second bottle when the first one finished.

As we ate, we talked, not only about the two murders. I learned that the inspector – 'call me Luca' – had only recently been promoted to Inspector and I could tell that he was keen. I asked him if he had heard anything from the pathologist yet, and he told me she had promised him something before the end of the afternoon. I also asked if there was any chance I might be able to take a look at the report on Beck's murder and he immediately agreed. As a result, we decided that I would come down to his office in the *questura* at four when we could go through everything together, drawing up a shortlist of people to be interviewed in more depth next morning. Hopefully by then, he might have heard from the pathologist and some more detailed information about the different guests might have come in from foreign police forces. In the meantime, I promised I would try to contact my 'friend' at MI6 – I didn't name him – in the hope that he might be able to tell me more about Beck, either on the record or off it.

I waited until I had left the camp and was out on the open hilltop with Oscar, far from prying ears, before making the call to Graham Oldman-Davis. After ten years, I half expected to find that the number was no longer recognised but, somewhat to my surprise, I heard it ring. It was answered almost immediately by a familiar voice.

'Inspector Armstrong, what a pleasant surprise.' My name must have appeared as one of his contacts. His patrician accent was as silky as ever, but I knew that it could just as easily turn to cold and calculating. He had always reminded me of a cat: elegant and tranquil one moment, ready to tear your eyes out the next. I remembered meeting him for the first time and thinking to myself that I was grateful we were both on the same side.

'Good afternoon, Mr Oldman-Davis, I hope I'm not disturbing you.'

'Always a pleasure to speak to you, Inspector. I hope you're keeping well.'

'Yes, thank you, and the same to you.' I decided to take a chance. 'I do hope your son's also doing well.'

'He's doing very well, thank you. He went back to university, got his degree and he's now working in the City. Much of that is down to you and I'll always be grateful for what you did for him.'

In fact, I hadn't done all that much. Ten years earlier, I'd been contacted by my superiors, who had in turn been contacted by people very high up in the government who had been concerned to hear that the son of an important member of the security services had been seen consorting with some very dubious company and dabbling with some nasty substances. Together with my sergeant, I had located him, removed him from the very insalubrious squat in which he had been living and returned him to the bosom of his family but, most importantly, we had managed to do it discreetly and without the news ever reaching the media. The last I'd heard of him had been that he had been shunted off to a rehab clinic deep in the depths of the Hampshire countryside. Hopefully, his father's buoyant reply to my question indicated that the lad had got his act together and I was pleased for him, and for his father. I hastened to take advantage of his cheerfulness and told him why I was calling. Conscious that I wasn't on an encrypted line, I chose my words carefully.

'I'm no longer working in London. I took early retirement and I'm now living in Italy. I'm currently on the Italian Riviera and I've heard about a suspicious death. I may be wrong, but it would appear that maybe you knew him. You may already have heard.' I deliberately didn't mention MI6 or the world of espionage.

He answered immediately, his tone instantly much more businesslike. 'I see. This is a terrible line, most unreliable.' He added a bit of extra emphasis to the final word and even Oscar could have taken the hint that it wasn't safe to discuss such matters openly. 'Tell me, whereabouts are you?' I told him and he made a suggestion. 'As it happens, I'm not very far from where you are. I'm staying with some friends just a bit further along the coast from you in France. Do you know Menton?'

'I've never been there but I know of it.' Menton was just on the other side of the French border, on the Côte d'Azur, not far from Monte Carlo.

'What are you doing for dinner this evening?'

'No plans.'

'Well, why don't you pop over and join me? There's an excellent restaurant I know just outside town. That way, we can talk without being interrupted.'

'If you're sure I'm not disturbing you, that would be excellent. Thank you so much.'

He promised to text me the name of the restaurant and directions as to how to get there and we agreed to meet there at eight. Barely two minutes after the call finished, a text arrived from him. I checked the restaurant out on the Internet and saw that it was one of the very few restaurants in the world to boast three Michelin stars for fine dining. No doubt the prices would be astronomical but that wasn't my immediate problem. It was quite clear that the only dogs allowed in a place like that would be guide dogs, so as soon as I got back to the tower, I explained the problem to Leo – telling him that I'd been invited out for dinner by simply 'an old friend' and without revealing that this would involve a trip over the border into France. In spite of my opaqueness, he was quick to offer to help out.

'You can leave Oscar with me. He'll be okay with me, won't he?'

'After the feast you gave him yesterday, he's definitely your friend for life. That would be great, thanks. I'm sorry to take advantage of you like this, but it's a guy I used to know when I was in the police who might even be able to help.' That was as far as I was going to go with details and he didn't quiz me further.

At four o'clock, as agreed, I drove down into the town to see the inspector. The *questura* occupied a relatively modern block a couple of streets back from the seafront. When I arrived at the front desk and asked for Inspector Sartori, I saw the officer behind the desk give Oscar a dubious look, but a minute later, Sergeant Rossi arrived and made a fuss of him before ushering us both upstairs. My friend Inspector Virgilio Pisano's office in Florence has an impressive view over the mighty bulk of the sixteenth-century Fortezza da Basso but Luca Sartori's view wasn't too bad either – certainly better than the view out of my window at Scotland Yard straight into the back of another building. Luca's window looked eastwards up the hillside on the eastern side of the valley, towards a headland topped by a little white chapel with an almost Byzantine dome, standing out against the azure blue of the sky.

Luca was seated behind a desk piled high with paperwork and the scene looked very familiar to me. He picked up one of the files as I came in and held it out towards me.

'*Ciao*, Dan. This is the Joseph Beck file from last weekend. As you can see, it isn't very thick.' I took it from him, noting that he was no longer using the formal form of the pronoun 'you' in Italian when he addressed me, so this was clear evidence that I had been accepted as part of the team.

I flipped it open and found only four sheets of paper and a handful of photos of the body and the location. There was a timeline indicating action taken from the moment the emergency call had come in at 0637 on Sunday morning through until 'No further action' at 1755 the same day. It added absolutely nothing to what I already knew. No background research had been done on the victim and the only attempt to notify next of kin had been a call to a telephone number at the back of his passport and a message left on an answer phone. I closed the file and handed it back to Luca.

'As you say, pretty slim. What about now? Has the pathologist sent in her report?'

He nodded. 'Yes, she's done a full autopsy on both bodies and the results are interesting. She's now able to confirm what she said earlier that both victims were rendered unconscious by a blow with a rounded implement – doubtless the steel bars from the gym – and then dropped into the pool where the back of the head was smashed into the stone edge so as to give the impression of an accident, before being left to drown. Both men had a considerable amount of alcohol in their systems and there was another empty whisky bottle lying in the bushes near this latest victim. She made a particularly interesting discovery when she examined the contents of the stomach of the first victim, Joseph Beck. Amongst all the stuff in there, she found a piece of broken tooth. This matched exactly with one of the victim's front teeth and she feels sure this must have been damaged when somebody was force-feeding him with alcohol, presumably after knocking him out. No question that we're looking at two murders and almost certainly the same perpetrator in both cases.'

'Any prints or DNA on the latest whisky bottle?'

'Only the victim's, just like Saturday night.'

'Was it the same brand as the first?'

He nodded. 'Just the same: Johnnie Walker Red Label.'

'What about prints or DNA on the murder weapons?'

He shook his head. 'Nothing at all. Both wiped clean.'

This made me think. 'With what? Assuming that both the murderer and the victims had been naked, what might have been used to clean the weapons? Yes, the killer could have washed them in the pool, but there would still have been prints from where he was holding them. Maybe he was wearing gloves but, if so, what did he do with the gloves afterwards? Alternatively, if he or she had brought a towel or an item of clothing along with them with the specific task of being used to clean the murder weapons, where did that end up?' I made a suggestion. 'I imagine you have people searching all the rubbish bins at the Retreat but you might like to tell them to be on the lookout not just for discarded gloves but maybe a piece of blood-stained cloth or clothing. Anything's possible.' I cast my mind back to the poolside and tried to think of anything there that might have been suitable for use to clean a murder weapon and an idea came to me. 'The parasol. There's a red umbrella by the pool where the life-guard sits. Presumably, that's closed at night and there would have been loose material flapping about. Maybe if you get your people to check that, they might find traces of the victims' blood and, if we're really lucky, some of the killer's DNA.'

Luca immediately instructed Rossi to get onto it and to speak to the officers checking the bins. The sergeant went out and the inspector picked up another file.

'We're gradually receiving background information on the people here at the Retreat but it's taking time to hear back from the different police forces in all the different countries. Nothing we've received so far stands out, although we have yet to hear back from Germany, and unfortunately the majority of the guests are German. None of those we've heard about so far have crim-inal history or convictions apart from a few speeding tickets.'

I took the files from him and started with the first victim but learned absolutely nothing more about Joseph Beck than what I had seen on the photocopy of his passport. No doubt whoever in London had responded to the request for information from the Italian police had come up against the same impenetrable barrier restricting access to the file as Paul had done. Hopefully, I might be able to penetrate that barrier when I dined with 'God' this evening.

The report on Owen Griffiths was slightly fuller but shed little fresh light. He had been born into a very wealthy family connected with the steel industry in South Wales and was a rich man with time on his hands. Never married, no convictions, nothing much to say about him. I looked up at Luca.

'Have you got the passports of the two victims? Could I have a look?'

He produced them from a drawer and I flicked through them. These were slightly more informative. Owen Griffiths appeared to have been a serial tourist and his passport was absolutely jam-packed with visas and entry/exit stamps for countries as far apart as Peru and Japan. However, as far as I could see, he'd never been to any potentially interesting countries from an espionage point of view like Russia, Iran or North Korea, so I handed his passport back and took a closer look at Beck's. This was the complete opposite. It had been issued only three months earlier and there wasn't a single stamp on any of the pages apart from his entry to the EU at Nice airport on the eleventh of May. I checked every page but there was nothing. Finally, I handed the passport back to Luca.

'I certainly can't see anything there to connect the two victims and I'm increasingly convinced that Griffiths was murdered because of something he'd seen, or something he claimed to have seen.'

Luca nodded. 'I agree.' He gave a frustrated sigh. 'I just hope when we get all the rest of the background information in on everybody currently at the Retreat that we pick something up because otherwise, I'm stuck.'

'Maybe I'll be able to find out something tonight.' I went on to tell him that I was meeting 'my friend from the UK security services' over the border in France this evening. 'I've no idea if he'll be able to give me any information of interest, but it's worth a try.'

13

THURSDAY EVENING

I set off at six-thirty and arrived at the restaurant with time to spare. The motorway crossed seamlessly into France through a short tunnel and the traffic wasn't too heavy. The hotel/restaurant itself occupied a magnificent villa high up the rocky *corniche* behind Menton and the view from the car park over the seaside town, home to the rich and famous, was spectacular, with the deep ultramarine of the Mediterranean flecked with a violet hue as the rays of the setting sun caught it. I drove past a selection of Ferraris, Lamborghinis and other supercars before finding a less conspicuous parking space around the side between a Peugeot van with the name of the hotel emblazoned on its side and a silver Mercedes sports car. At least here I was well out of sight. I had a feeling the management would probably take a dim view of my ten-year-old van with its scratches and dents.

From a security point of view, the place was ideal, with just the one road leading to it up a series of hairpin bends. There would be little chance of an opportunistic thief or somebody with more sinister intent being able to make a clean getaway before the police had time to set up a roadblock down below. I had little doubt that 'God', in the shape of Mr Oldman-Davis, had deliberately engineered our meeting with security in mind. But of course, that was his stock in trade.

I got out of the van, taking care not to touch the Mercedes beside me, noticing that the glass of the wing mirror was badly cracked – and I knew how expensive they are to replace. I hoped the driver wouldn't try to blame that on me. Stretching, I walked to the edge of the car park, from where I could look down the steeply sloping hillside towards the town and the sea. It was an atmospheric view and I took a photo and sent it to Anna with a very short message.

Thinking of you and looking forward to bringing you here later this month. x

Whether she would still be talking to me by then remained uncertain.

I waited until five to eight and then went in. I had showered and changed into a clean shirt and long trousers before setting off, as I suspected it might turn out to be the kind of place where the men would be in tuxedos and the women in evening gowns, sparkling with jewels. My first impression appeared to confirm that; even the doorman was better dressed than I was. It was therefore a considerable relief when I was shown into the sumptuous lounge bar to see that most of the other guests were casually dressed. When I say casually, I don't mean cheaply. Even though I have no knowledge of high fashion – as already pointed out to me by Freddie – I could see that the people around me didn't buy their clothes at their local supermarket.

As I stood at the doorway, looking around the discreetly luxurious interior, a figure materialised silently at my side. I turned to see that this was a fit-looking man with close-cropped, fair hair, wearing a dark-blue blazer and immaculately pressed, light-grey trousers. He gave me a polite nod of the head and spoke just loud enough for me to hear. 'The boss is waiting for you outside.' His accent was definitely English but almost neutral, hard to place.

Without waiting for my response, he headed for glazed doors at the far end of the room and I followed obediently. I've come across enough spooks in my time to recognise one when I see one. I wondered just exactly who these 'friends' were with whom my host claimed to be staying. Certainly, if he had brought backup, this probably wasn't quite what most people would describe as a holiday. Still, that was his affair and, no doubt, the affair of the British government, and I certainly wasn't going to ask.

The glass doors opened onto a magnificent terrace with a panoramic view along the coast back towards Italy. Tables were set up out here, discreetly distanced one from another and separated by huge, terracotta urns overflowing with flowers, all of them shaded from the sun beneath a wrought-iron pergola intertwined with a magnificent display of purple bougainvillaea. I followed the man in the blazer past a series of tables, at one of which I was sure I recognised a household name Formula One driver dining with a pair of immensely beautiful women. Finally, we reached the end table at the far corner of the terrace and here I saw the familiar face of Graham Oldman-Davis. He was going a bit grey at the temples – but I'm a fine one to talk – but otherwise, he looked unchanged. As he spotted me, he rose to his feet and held out his hand in greeting.

'Inspector Armstrong, sorry, *Chief* Inspector Armstrong, it's good to see you again.' He glanced up at my shadow, who melted away without a word being spoken. 'God' was on his own at a table set for two. There was a bottle of champagne sticking out of an ice bucket on a separate little table alongside and as we both sat down, a uniformed waiter appeared from nowhere, opened the bottle with only the slightest hiss and poured the champagne into our two glasses before disappearing again. 'God' picked his glass up and held it out towards me. 'Cheers, Mr Armstrong.'

'Cheers, and thanks for seeing me so quickly.'

'Like I said, it's good to meet up with you again. I understand that you now have your own detective agency in Florence.' Clearly he had been doing his homework. 'Now that's a beautiful city, isn't it? I rather envy you living there.'

We exchanged trivialities about life in Tuscany before he set his glass down and leant forward on his elbows towards me.

'I assume you've come to see me about Beck.'

'That's correct. You will have heard that he's dead but you maybe haven't heard that he was murdered.'

His face gave nothing away but, even so, I got the impression that this didn't come as a surprise to him and I wondered how he had heard. All he did was nod, so I continued. 'He was struck over the head with a blunt object some time between 10 p.m. and midnight last Saturday and his body was then put in the swimming pool of a naturist retreat not far from Alassio. Attempts were made to try to make it look like an accident but the pathologist has now confirmed that it was definitely murder. The reason I've come to you is to ask for your help in trying to discover why he was murdered and by whom.'

He took a mouthful of his champagne and I could see him swirl it around his mouth while he considered his response. Finally, he swallowed and looked straight across the table at me. He had cold, hard, light-blue eyes, and I felt them boring into me.

'Can I ask how you come to be involved in this affair? Surely murder is a police matter.'

I explained how I had been contacted by a woman I had once jailed, whose father was the owner of the camp where the murder had happened. I told him I'd been hired to investigate and I was now assisting the local police. It came as no surprise when he then asked the same questions that I had asked.

'Who is this man and who's the woman who claims to be his daughter, for that matter? Why is he so convinced it was murder when the police were not?'

'That's a very good question. The man in question is an Italo American called Leonardo 'Leo' Moretti, and his daughter's called Bianca. The answer he gave me was simply that he liked the guy who was killed. I've no reason to believe he had anything to do with the murder, but there's something deep down inside of me telling me that he and his daughter know more than they're letting on.'

I saw him digest my words and I had to wait almost a minute for him to start speaking again. 'Mr Armstrong, I trust you and I have good reason to be grateful to you. What I'm going to tell you is for your ears only, and even the Italian police should only be told the bare minimum. Is that clear?'

'I give you my word.'

'Joseph Beck was born Josef Beck.' He pronounced Beck's first name the German way as if it started with a Y. 'He was born in Chemnitz, Germany in 1977. Are you familiar with the city?' I shook my head and he elaborated. 'The city is in Saxony in the eastern part of Germany and at the end of the Second World War, it fell into Soviet hands and became part of the DDR, East Germany. In 1953, the DDR authorities renamed the city Karl-Marx-Stadt and it retained that name until the fall of the Berlin Wall in 1989 and the collapse of the Soviet Union in 1991, after which the name was changed back to the original. In other words, Beck was born in a city under Soviet control, exercised with an iron fist through the East German secret police, the Stasi. You may have heard of them.' He stopped and took a mouthful of champagne. 'I apologise if you already know all this but the background is important, I can assure you.'

I had heard the infamous name, Stasi, before but the rest was new to me. 'I'm fascinated. Please go on.'

'Beck's father, Heinrich, was a journalist and a free thinker and, as such, he was a thorn in the side of the establishment. He was arrested and imprisoned on a number of occasions before finally, the Stasi lost patience with him and he was picked up on the street and beaten so badly that he died before he got to hospital. That was in 1987, when Josef was only ten. His mother could see the writing on the wall and knew that she and her son had to get out fast. By a variety of means – some of which were engineered by friends of ours, and the details of which remain classified – she made her way to what should have been a weak spot in the border between East and West Germany. She and the boy attempted to escape along a tried and tested route but almost immediately were picked up by searchlights and the guards opened fire, hitting both of them. The mother died instantly but somehow, despite a serious stomach wound, the boy managed to crawl through the wire and was picked up by colleagues of mine and rushed to hospital, more dead than alive. It would seem that the authorities had been tipped off that an escape attempt would be made and they were waiting for them.'

I nodded, still fascinated. This, of course, explained the scar on Beck's belly. I listened, spellbound, as my dinner companion continued.

'Young Josef spent a long time in hospital in West Germany and then was brought over to the UK, where he was placed in a foster family: fine people who quickly recognised his potential. He learned English with ease, did brilliantly at school and obtained British citizenship at age eighteen. He demonstrated a rare talent for languages and was awarded a bursary to Balliol to study modern languages. It was while he was there that we approached him to work for us. He turned out to be one of our best agents and he will be sorely missed.' He glanced over my shoulder and nodded to somebody in the background. 'Now, before we go any further, maybe we should order our dinner. If you're omnivorous, I can heartily recommend the *menu gastronomique*. Maybe with a bottle of Meursault? How does that sound?'

'That sounds perfect, thank you.' I waited while he gave the slightest of nods of the head to whoever was lurking in the shadows behind me and that appeared to be sufficient. When I had his attention again, I asked the obvious question. 'Can you tell me, please, whether you think his murder is connected with his work or whether it might be a personal matter? It would appear that he was a bit of a ladies' man, so there's always the possibility that jealousy may have been the motive.'

He smiled. 'A *bit* of a ladies' man? Was Albert Einstein a *bit* of a scientist? Was Aristotle a *bit* of a philosopher? Beck was insatiable. His history with the service is littered with broken-hearted women and cuckolded husbands. Any one of them could have done it.'

'So you're saying you think it was a crime of passion?'

'I'm just putting it out there as a possibility.' There was a pregnant pause before he spoke again. 'There are other possibilities, however. All his life since coming to the UK, Beck had one idea in his head and that was to find out who betrayed his mother and himself to the authorities and tipped off the guards when he and she made their attempted escape. I understand from my sources that this naturist camp has quite a large contingent of German nationals. I wonder whether he went there deliberately looking for somebody he suspected and that person, or somebody acting on their behalf, decided to kill him rather than run the risk of being discovered.'

I couldn't help wondering who his 'sources' might be who knew so much about the Retreat but, for now, I ignored that. The German connection was intriguing and certainly a completely new line of inquiry. Could it really be that Beck's murder had been provoked by events over thirty years earlier? That, of course, did little to provide a motive for the second murder unless, as I had been thinking, that had been to eliminate a potential witness to the first killing. Certainly, as far as I could see, Owen Griffiths had had no links with British intelligence.

Or had he? After all, an unprepossessing almost-sixty-year-old flitting around the world as a tourist would probably have provided pretty good cover. No sooner had I thought this than it occurred to me that I was also a soon-to-be-sixty-year old and I was still plying the detective trade, so maybe the tourist thing might really have been cover for Griffiths, the spy. I had no chance to press 'God' on the subject because at that moment, our hors d'oeuvres arrived.

This was the task of two waiters. A plate was set in front of each of us, each covered by a gleaming, silver dome, and then, in a perfectly synchronised movement, both covers were removed with a flourish and one of the waiters intoned gravely, 'Araignée de mer avec asperges vertes truffées,' before retiring into the shadows.

Remarkably, my A-level French from many years ago allowed me to translate reasonably well even though I couldn't at first think what 'sea spiders' were. Fortunately, my dinner companion was more familiar with fine dining here in France than I was.

'Excellent, I do so love spider crab. And asparagus has always been one of my favourites.'

I'd had spider crab many years ago on holiday with my ex-wife in

Greece and I could remember it taking the best part of an hour with a variety of implements from a hammer to a skewer to crack my way through the long, thin legs and retrieve what little meat there was to be found on it. It had been tasty but exhausting. Tonight, the chef had already done the hard work for us and I was presented with a plate with two perfectly symmetrical, round blobs, each about the size of a scone, one a creamy colour and one fairly lurid bright green. A swirl of some kind of brown sauce – not the kind you find in a bottle at a greasy spoon café – completed the appearance of the dish, which was far more sophisticated than my attempt to describe it.

I imagine it's a reflection on my plebeian background, but I've never really been that fussed about fancy food, but I suspended my disbelief and set about the crab and the asparagus and I had to admit that the combination of tastes was quite amazing. Maybe there was something in this haute cuisine business after all. Not for the first time this evening, I found myself hoping I wouldn't be presented with the bill at the end of this meal. It probably would have swallowed every cent of the freshly minted euros paid to me by Bianca Moretti.

I made a couple of tentative efforts to return the conversation to the subject of the double murders, but I rapidly got the feeling that my dinner companion took a dim view of mixing business with pleasure so I soon gave up. In spite of my probably totally unfounded prejudices, the meal was a real delight. The exquisite hors d'oeuvres were followed by fillets of turbot laced with caviar and then a main course of caramelised duck breast with a water-cress and green pear coulis. After a few pieces of cheese from a massive platter heaving with about thirty different varieties, resting on top of something the size of a shopping trolley, we ended the meal with crêpes filled with a Madagascar vanilla sauce and the most amazing crunchy, tiny cubes of grapefruit.

Finally, as we sat back and sipped our Lavazza coffees – the

only nod to the fact that Italy was barely four or five miles away –
I managed to bring my host back to the matter in hand.

'Does the name Owen Griffiths mean anything to you? A
Welshman in his late fifties.'

He shook his head. 'No, should it?'

'Not necessarily. It's just that there has been a second murder
at the camp and I've been trying to establish if there's a connection between the two.'

'I'm afraid I can't help. He certainly wasn't one of ours. Maybe
he was killed because he saw something on Saturday night.'

'That's what I'm coming round to thinking. If I understand
you correctly, you think there might be a choice of motives for
Beck's murder. So far, we have either jealousy involving a woman
or some hang back to the events of 1987. You mentioned a *number*
of possible scenarios. Could it be something else? Could I ask
what sort of work he'd been doing recently?' I was quick to add a
disclaimer. 'I know you can't give me details, but could you just
give me your opinion as to whether he might have been involved
with anything particularly sensitive that might have resulted in
somebody being sent after him?'

Before answering, he raised a finger and, just like that, a
waiter appeared by the table. 'I must admit, I feel like a good
brandy. Will you join me?'

I shook my head. 'Thank you but, much as I'd like to, I have to
drive afterwards so I'd better not, but don't let me stop you.'

I heard him ask for a twenty-year-old Napoleon and the
waiter disappeared as silently as he had come. Only then did my
host reply to my question. 'You're quite right, that's the other
possible motive. As you say, I can't give you any details but I can
tell you that Beck had been working closely with our American
cousins on a complex operation involving a multibillion-dollar
drug cartel operating across Europe and the US. I'm afraid that's

the most I can tell you. Certainly, that involves some very nasty people with some huge vested interests, and they would have had no scruples about sending a hitman after him but, as far as we know, his cover hadn't been blown so that remains unlikely. I hope that helps but, if I was a betting man – and in fact, I am – I would suggest that, as they say here in France, your best bet would be to *cherchez la femme*.'

14

FRIDAY MORNING

Oscar woke me at seven with a prod of his nose so I got up and went downstairs with him for his morning walk. In the living room, I found Leo doing something on his laptop and I wondered if he ever got any sleep. When I had got back to the tower the previous night at almost midnight, he had still been up and I'd subsequently found him sitting there watching the TV when I'd returned with Oscar from his late-night stroll. I hadn't told him where I'd been or the identity of my dinner companion and he'd been very circumspect, asking me only if the meeting had gone well. In response, all I had told him had been that it was looking more and more likely that the first murder had been committed either by a woman scorned or a jealous partner. I made no mention of the German or the drug connection. As for Owen Griffiths' murder, I told Leo that this had most likely been an attempt to liquidate a potential witness to the first killing.

Leo seemed more interested in what I'd had to eat and he nodded appreciatively as I reeled off the list of dishes. At my feet, I noticed my Labrador following my words intently. As already established, when it comes to food, Oscar's comprehension skills are unrivalled. When Leo asked me for the name of the restaurant, I decided to dissimulate and told him it had been a French restaurant in Sanremo and that I would dig out the name and let him have it, but with no intention of doing anything of the kind. At the end of the meal last night, no bill had been presented and my offer to contribute had been waved away by 'God' – much to my relief. I was increasingly convinced that this might mean that he was a guest there along with his bodyguard and possibly other members of the security service, and I felt it wiser not to divulge his whereabouts to anybody, not even Leo. I still hadn't forgotten my impression that Bianca had known more than she'd told me when she'd come to my office and, by extension, this cast a shadow over her father, whose answers to some of my questions had been less than convincing. In the murky world of intelligence, discretion is always the best policy.

When I went over to the Retreat that Friday morning, the police were already there in force. I gave Inspector Sartori a slightly fuller version of the previous night's meeting – still without naming my host – although I kept my promise not to reveal more than the briefest details of our discussion. 'My source confirms that Beck was indeed working for MI6, British Intelligence, and there's a possibility there might be a link to events in East Germany thirty-five years ago. Alternatively, he told me Beck's recently been involved in a big drug investigation, so it could be it was a professional hit, but his gut feeling, knowing what sort of man Beck was, was that the odds are more in favour of it having been a crime of passion.'

Luca thanked me and ran through his plans for the day. He told me he'd now received background information from the German authorities about the German nationals currently here at the Retreat and a quick study of these had revealed nothing that, to his mind, added any further suspects to our shortlist. In consequence, he intended to have a second interview in the course of the morning with those we had deemed potentially suspicious in the hope that by applying a bit more pressure, he might be able to squeeze more information out of one or more of them. While this was going on, he would arrange for the accommodation of each of them to be carefully searched and for fingerprints and DNA samples to be taken. He asked me to sit in on the interviews with him and to help with interpreting, as well as asking my own questions if I so chose. I agreed readily and asked if I could take a look at the report from Germany first.

While he went down to the pool to meet up with Sergeant Rossi, I sat down at a table and opened the file from Germany. It had very helpfully been written in English and, although it didn't go into much detail, it produced a pretty good sketch of each of the guests. As Luca had said, there was nobody with any significant criminal record. Remembering what my dinner companion last night had said about the German connection, I checked each of the entries for any mention of Chemnitz or Karl-Marx-Stadt, but without finding anything. In particular, I paid special attention to the three Germans we were going to interview for a second time later this morning.

Hans and Petra Muller were from Frankfurt, where he worked as a vet and she as a veterinary assistant. They had been married for fourteen years, had no children, and appeared to be an ideal couple. Both of them were in their late forties and both had looked fit in yesterday's interviews, but I remembered that both of them had appeared unexpectedly stressed. The husband in particular had had sweat beading on his brow and running down the sides of his face and he'd kept wiping himself with his palms. Another of the disadvantages of naturism is that there's nowhere to keep a tissue. I wondered what, apart from a lack of a tissue, had been so worrying for the couple. A guilty conscience, perhaps?

The other German to be called in for a second interview was Klaus Schinken. According to the report, he came from a small town just outside Dresden – formerly part of the DDR. He was sixty-five years old and a shopkeeper. During the first interview, he had appeared relatively relaxed and I had a feeling the inspector was only calling him back because the man was travelling on his own. As far as any connection with Joseph or Josef Beck was concerned, back in 1987, Schinken would have been in his thirties so possibly the age of a policeman or border guard. The fact was, however, that there was no mention of him having a background in the police force or local government and this made me think that the chances of him having been involved in the tragic escape attempt were unlikely, but I resolved to check with him anyway.

When Luca and the sergeant returned, they brought news.

'Well done, Dan. Sure enough, when my people ran a blue light over the red parasol, they very quickly located faint bloodstains. I've sent the whole umbrella off to the lab in the hope that we may be able to get some of the perpetrator's DNA. As soon as we've got samples from all the people we're interviewing again this morning, we can try comparing them. Here's hoping.'

I was delighted, but I sounded a note of caution. 'The trouble is, there were no prints on either of the steel bars so the perpetrator was either wearing gloves or had found some other way of gripping the murder weapon and then throwing it over the fence.' A thought occurred to me. 'It might be a good idea if you tell your people when they search each of the suspects' accommodation and belongings that they check every item of clothing and every towel with a UV light just in case the killer brought something with them to use for holding the weapon. I remember a case once where the murderer used a sock to cover the handle of the hammer when he bludgeoned the victim to death and then threw the hammer into the Thames, hanging onto the sock. Stupidly, he then put it back on again and, when we picked him up later that night, the faint traces of blood on the sock incriminated him.'

Luca nodded to Sergeant Rossi, who went off to relay the instruction. I handed Luca back the German file and asked about the other suspects on this morning's schedule. 'Have you heard back from the Hungarians or the Czech authorities, or the UK authorities for that matter?'

'Yes, yes and, strangely, no. Normally your compatriots are very quick at getting back to us in response to requests for information.'

'That *is* strange. Maybe there's a problem. Could I see the reports on the Hungarians and the Czech?'

Luca handed me two sheets of paper and I looked them over. The Czech man, Adam Novotny, born in Karlovy Vary in the west of the Czech Republic, was forty-two, and when we had interviewed him the previous day, he had struck all of us as a bit strange. This didn't necessarily mean that we thought he was a murderer, but his manner had been shifty and from time to time, we had noticed an expression on his face that might have been guilt. Alternatively, it might just have been digestive problems or natural anxiety at being interviewed in connection with a murder. Under 'Occupation', it just said 'state employee'. That could cover a broad spectrum from postman to hitman, so we needed to find out exactly what he did.

The Hungarian couple, Laszlo and Maria Farkas, were both in their late thirties and had been married for seven years. He was described as being a fitness trainer and she as a clerk. Once again, we needed to find out more about them, although from his body-builder physique, likened by the inspector to Arnold

Schwarzenegger, fitness trainer seemed like a pretty logical occupation.

The shortlist of potential suspects started with the two English couples, and the inspector very sensibly decided to interview each person individually. Jeremy Smith was called in first and he arrived looking slightly less sunburned than the previous day, but still distinctly pink rather than brown. I got the impression he wasn't an outdoorsman. Now that I was seeing him with a bit more leisure than at yesterday's marathon preliminary interview session, there was something familiar about him. It wasn't that I'd met him before, but he belonged to a type I'd come up against on numerous occasions in the course of my career at the Met. The adjective that immediately came to mind was 'dodgy'. He didn't look in the least bit fazed by the fact that he'd been called back for a second interview in a murder investigation and he sat opposite us with just a hint of an insolent smile on his face throughout. Somehow, I knew in my bones that this wasn't the first time he'd been questioned by the police.

When the inspector asked what he did for a living, his answer was laconic.

'Manager.'

'Of what?'

'A club.' Clearly, getting information out of him wasn't going to be simple.

'What sort of club?'

'A *club* club, you know, a place people go to for drinks and to meet friends.' His tone was mocking.

This definition could apply to a broad spectrum of locales from the local Conservative Club to the raunchiest strip club. As he had given his address as being in South East London where I had spent my early years in the force, I pressed him to be more specific, and when he grudgingly gave me the name and address of the club, I recognised it immediately.

'The Green Parrot? I thought that place was closed down years ago.'

For the first time, he looked mildly fazed. 'You know it?'

'I knew it until we closed it down for multiple licensing and drug violations. Does this mean it's reopened?'

'When you say "we" closed it down, who are you? Are you police as well?' He was sounding less sure of himself now so I decided a little white lie might help me capitalise on this.

'Yes, Metropolitan Police murder squad.' Seeing that this had the desired effect of wiping the sneer off his face, I upped the ante. 'We're taking these murders very seriously.' If he wanted to infer from this that I'd been sent over from London specially, then that might help to loosen his tongue.

Inspector Sartori shot me a surreptitious wink and picked up the questioning again. 'Please can you tell me how you chose this place for your holiday? Do you regularly go to naturist camps?'

Smith shook his head. 'No, this is the first time. A friend in London recommended we should try it so I suggested it to Lorraine and she was all for it.'

'And is she still enthusiastic?'

He nodded. 'We both are. It's a great place they have here.'

I very nearly pitched in to ask why, if she was loving it so much, his girlfriend had a face like a wet weekend, but I decided to put that to her directly when we interviewed her next. The inspector asked a few more questions, pressing him on whether he had known either of the victims, but Smith just shook his head and denied any contact with either of them. Finally, the inspector dismissed him and, after the door had closed, he and I exchanged looks.

'I think it's safe to say that your fiction about still working for the Metropolitan Police definitely worried him. I just hope we get his background report from your people in London as soon as possible because it wouldn't surprise me if he has a record.'

I nodded in agreement. 'My feelings entirely. I'll get onto another of my old friends in London and check up on the Green Parrot club. It used to be a real dive and we regularly arrested members of staff as well as customers, mainly for dealing drugs but also a number of more serious offences. Maybe it's turned over a new leaf but, if not, then I think our friend Mr Smith is going to need close watching.'

Next to be interviewed was Smith's girlfriend, Lorraine Hickson. Close up, she was a good-looking woman with a mass of blonde hair. However, it was interesting to see that in spite of her being stark naked, she had still taken the time to apply a liberal coating of make-up. In consequence, her pasty face with its cherry-red lips looked as if it had been attached to the wrong body. She was looking more nervous than her boyfriend but I got the impression this had nothing to do with her lack of clothing. In fact, if this really was her first experience of naturism, she appeared remarkably unbothered, even though she was in the presence of three fully clothed men.

Luca ran through the same questions he had asked her boyfriend and we discovered that although she initially said that she was a waitress, it soon emerged that she was actually a dancer, and a specific kind of dancer at that. Her lack of concern at her nudity was explained when she revealed she was a pole dancer. I asked her where she performed and it came as no surprise to hear the name of the club. In my day, the Green Parrot had been a disco but now it had apparently moved either up or down in the world – depending on how one felt about such things – reinventing itself as a lap-dancing establishment. She told us she had worked there for three years, but when asked how long she and Jeremy Smith had been an item, her answer was far from convincing.

'Ages.'

'What are we talking, Lorraine? Days, weeks, months?'

She clearly had to think about this and her answer, when it came, was unconvincing. 'Six months, a year, I forget.'

'And the two of you get on well together?'

She nodded her head but it was a pretty poor bit of acting. I tried to press her on how things were between her and Jeremy but she suddenly became monosyllabic and by the time she left, we had learned very little detail about their relationship apart from the fact that, not only were things not going swimmingly between them, but I had definitely got the feeling that she might even be afraid of him.

Now why might that be?

15

FRIDAY MORNING

The interviews continued with the other British couple. Oliver Harcourt came in and sat down, ramrod straight, his arms crossed in front of him. He looked quite unperturbed and he answered all our questions with apparent ease, his accent posh Home Counties English. No, neither he nor his wife had met the first victim and contact with the second had not extended further than hello and goodbye on a couple of occasions. On both Saturday and Wednesday night, he and his wife had eaten here at the restaurant and then had retired to bed at just after ten. Although on the face of it, he appeared cooperative and helpful, I still couldn't shake the feeling that he wasn't telling us the whole truth, but maybe I was just prejudiced by his autocratic demeanour.

I asked him about his military background and he confirmed that he had been in the Grenadier Guards for twenty-five years, retiring five years earlier with the rank of lieutenant colonel. His left forearm bore what looked like his parachute wings and there was a more recent red and blue tattoo on the right arm. He tapped it with his fingers and produced a look of pride.

'Finest regiment in the world.'

He and his wife now lived near Haslemere in Surrey and he divided his time between his garden and the golf course. He sounded like a typical upper-middle class, blue-blooded Englishman. Maybe a bit too typical – although coming across a lieutenant-colonel with tattoos was unexpected. Somehow, I had always thought that sort of thing would have been frowned upon by the powers that be but maybe I was just old-fashioned. Certainly, in my day, tattoos for police officers had been banned – or at least well hidden.

His wife, Fleur, had the sort of over-the-top, syrupy accent that made my skin creep. She positively oozed upper-crust noblesse and, me being me, I took an instant dislike to her. She made quite clear that she had spoken to neither of the victims and the unspoken reason was that she had deemed them to be beneath her. When asked what she did for a living, she looked genuinely shocked before answering haughtily that she had had no need of employment. Why was she here in a naturist retreat? To get a fresh perspective on life, of course. Would I have bought a used car from her? Not on your life. Did I believe her or her husband capable of murder? Anything was possible.

She was followed by Hungarian man-mountain, Laszlo Farkas. When he came padding in, even Oscar looked up and stared. The guy was positively bulging with muscle and I swear I heard his inner thighs chafing as he walked, so bulky were his leg muscles. He sat down opposite us – the chair creaked but fortunately didn't buckle – and the inspector ran through the questions, during which we discovered that Laszlo was not only a fitness instructor in a Budapest leisure centre but also a former Olympic weightlifter. He told us his wife, Maria, also had a sporting background – as a sprinter – but it turned out she had never reached his dizzy heights. When we interviewed her, she told us she worked behind the reception desk at the same leisure centre so here, on the face of it, was another couple who worked together like Mr Smith and his lady friend. Neither she nor her husband seemed suspicious, although I got the feeling that maybe there was something they were holding back but, in spite of our best efforts, they didn't reveal anything significant. However, when asked if she had known either of the victims, Maria produced an interesting, if tantalising, piece of information.

'We never spoke to either of them but when Laszlo and I were walking back to our camper van late on Wednesday night, I'm sure I heard a woman's voice inside the cabin where the old Englishman was staying. Laszlo says he didn't hear a thing, but I'm quite sure *I* did. I remember it because it was the very first time I'd heard him speak to anybody.' She rolled her eyes. 'We reckoned he was a bit strange...'

Hearing Owen Griffiths, who had been almost exactly my age, being described as 'old' came as a bit of a blow to my self-esteem, but I did my best to rise above this as I reflected that this news was potentially important to the case. I tried to extract more information from her but she claimed that she had only heard a man's voice and a woman's voice but had seen neither of them as they had been inside the chalet. When asked if she had heard what they were saying, she shook her head. 'It sounded like English, but I couldn't make out any particular words.'

After she had left, Luca and I had a quick chat. It was interesting that he, too, had got the impression that these two weren't being completely open, but neither of us could put a finger on what it might be. She, certainly, would have made an unlikely killer – not least because she was probably at least a foot shorter than either of the two victims and would have struggled to reach up and club them. Her husband, on the other hand, could probably have snapped their necks with one hand. In consequence, I put a question mark alongside both of their names on my list for now.

We both agreed that the haughty English couple weren't particularly loveable but neither of us could envisage them being involved in violent murder, although there was still something about them that didn't convince me. Maybe the search of their belongings that was going on this morning would throw up a clue of some kind.

Next on the list was Adam Novotny from the Czech Republic. I remembered him from yesterday as being very subdued, very reticent and just a bit strange, but when he came in and sat down in front of us today, he looked more normal. He was forty-two years old with bright-ginger hair and his whole body was covered in freckles. He spoke remarkably good English and his fluency was explained by the fact that he was a secondary-school teacher of German and English. I couldn't help remembering some of the teachers at my old school, like 'Golfy' Brice who had worn plus fours and carried a golf club around the classroom with him, practising his swing as he fired questions at us. He used to smash this down hard on the desks of pupils he deemed inattentive and, on one memorable occasion, he had split the top of one wooden desk clean in half. In comparison to Golfy, Adam Novotny was the epitome of normality, not least when he explained his uncommunicative state the previous day.

'I must apologise for my behaviour yesterday, gentlemen. I'm afraid I was suffering from a severe hangover. I was playing online *Grand Theft Auto* until 2 a.m. and I drank far more than I should have done.' He shook his head ruefully. 'I didn't win.'

The inspector questioned his story. 'Yesterday, when we asked you what you were doing between nine and midnight on Wednesday night, you said you couldn't remember. How come you've changed your story?'

He looked suitably chastened. 'Like I say, I drank far too much and it took me until yesterday evening before it all came back to me. I'm sorry, I didn't mean to mislead you.'

He gave us details of the online game and the sergeant was instructed to double-check to see if anybody could recall him leaving at any time but as an alibi, it was tenuous. It wasn't as if it had been via a video link and I knew of at least three recent cases where resourceful perpetrators – a whole lot more computer savvy than I am – had attempted to manufacture alibis involving online games. Still, he disclaimed any knowledge of either victim and I couldn't immediately see how a Czech schoolteacher might be connected with a spy or a millionaire gadabout.

The next interviewees were the fashionistas. We interviewed Melinda Barker first but managed to get very little out of her except that she claimed to have had no contact with Owen Griffiths, although she did admit to having spoken to Joseph Beck a couple of times. We asked what this had been about, but she just waved her hand vaguely and replied, 'Stuff... the weather, that sort of thing.' When asked if she thought her roommate might have had some kind of liaison with Joseph Beck, she shook her head, but not before an expression crossed her face that looked very much to me as if it could have almost been jealousy. The inspector pressed her on this but she dug her heels in and claimed it was quite impossible. To underline her point, she looked straight at us and informed us in a tone that brooked no argument, 'Kim would never shack up with a man like him.'

She was followed by tall, beautiful Kim and this was where things got a bit more interesting. When the inspector quoted Melinda's last line to her, she nodded in agreement, and she managed to look pretty convincing. We now had quite a lot of evidence that she and Beck had been close and, although it took a little while and quite a lot of persuasion, she finally gave in and confessed that she and he had had what she described as 'a connection' over the course of the previous week but she went to great pains to spell out that nothing physical had happened between them. In fact, I even got the feeling that I could detect a note of regret in her voice. Had this lack of intimacy not been her choice? Although she had spent quite a lot of time with him during the days before his death, she claimed they had only been friends and that she had been in her chalet with Melinda all night on Saturday when he was killed. I asked her whether Melinda had been aware of her relationship with Beck and she shook her head – not altogether convincingly.

'No, I don't think so.'

'What do you think her reaction would have been if she'd found out you and he were close?'

'She wouldn't have minded. Besides, like I say, nothing happened between me and him.'

This did little to allay our suspicions that she or her room-mate might have murdered Beck, but we couldn't get her to reveal anything more – for now.

When she had left the room, the inspector snapped his note-book shut and stood up. 'Let's take a break. I need to check in with the office and see if there have been any developments, like the report from the UK police, for example. Shall we meet back here in half an hour?'

I stood up as well and, immediately, so did Oscar. I glanced down at him. 'Why don't you and I go for a little walk?'

In response, he headed for the door.

Outside on the hillside, I pulled out my phone and tried the number of my old boss in Lewisham from many years ago. He was well into his seventies now but his memory was still as sharp as a razor. When I mentioned the Green Parrot, he confirmed that it was now a strip club but the name Jeremy Smith meant nothing to him. I toyed with the idea of phoning Paul at Scotland Yard to ask him, but I'd already bothered him enough so I decided to wait for the official report from London to arrive on Luca's desk.

As Oscar and I wandered about, I found myself thinking about Joseph Beck. Everybody seemed convinced that he had been an inveterate womaniser but I had yet to find a woman who admitted to having had a physical relationship with him. What might this mean? I remembered an infamous case we had had five or six years earlier when I was still DCI Armstrong. This had involved a member of parliament who, in order to conceal the fact that he was gay, had quite successfully managed to get himself a reputation with the ladies only for it all subsequently to be revealed as a smokescreen.

Was that what Beck had been doing? But, if so, did that mean that 'God' had been lying when he'd told me the man was a womaniser or had Beck successfully pulled the wool over his boss's eyes as well? Besides, being gay carried no stigma these days in most countries of the world – although not all – and I couldn't see why he might be trying to hide this. I shook my head in annoyance. Maybe I was just overthinking things. My ex-wife had often accused me of doing that.

After a quick walk, I returned to the Retreat and the interviews recommenced. First on the list was Klaus Schinken.

Just like the previous day, the German appeared quite relaxed and the only new bit of information we got out of him was that he claimed to have seen Owen Griffiths with a woman on Wednesday at around ten o'clock. The two figures had been walking in the direction of Griffiths' chalet but Schinken was unable to provide a positive identification. All he said was that she'd had blonde hair and a nice bottom. He accompanied this last observation with a big grin and he was still grinning when he left the room. I looked across at Luca.

'He's either a good actor or he's completely innocent. If he's telling the truth, this corroborates what Maria Farkas said about Griffiths having had company. I wouldn't mind betting that this blonde woman was the bait to lure Griffiths to the pool and his death.'

Luca nodded. 'My thoughts entirely and we've already seen three blondes today, four if you include the haughty Mrs Harcourt, haven't we?' He smiled ruefully. 'At least this makes it less likely that the model was involved. Her hair's jet black.'

Always one to play devil's advocate, I felt I should query that. 'Unless her blonde roommate did the luring and Kim did the killing.'

Our next interviewee was also blonde. This was Petra Muller from Frankfurt, the veterinary assistant, and she confirmed our supposition that she worked with her husband in his veterinary practice. Just like the previous day, she was looking very nervous and I couldn't miss how her fingers kept drumming on her thigh as she spoke to us. Yes, a police interview can be nerve-wracking, but I was ever more convinced that she was hiding something. The inspector and I both tried several times to discover what might be behind her anxiety, but we got nothing out of her. In the end, Luca sent her away and we pinned our hopes on her husband, the vet.

Like the previous day, Hans Muller arrived in a right old state. Not only was there sweat running down the sides of his face, but I could also see it glistening on his torso as it ran down the rest of his body. It occurred to me that it would probably be a good idea to run a cloth over the seat after he left otherwise the next interviewee might well sit down and slide straight off it. I don't know whether it was some deep-rooted animal sixth sense, but when he walked in, Oscar, who's normally so friendly towards strangers, immediately got up and trotted around behind me so that he was protected by my body. He's not a fan of vets.

Luca started with the simple stuff. 'Did you or your wife have any contact with either of the victims?'

Muller immediately shook his head and I couldn't pick up even a hint of guilt on his face as he replied. 'No, neither of them. I saw the first victim swimming in the pool a few times, but we never spoke. As for the other guy, I'm not even too sure who he was: another Englishman, I believe.'

This all sounded pretty convincing but, if he had nothing to hide, why was he sweating like a pig? I tried a question of my own. 'Is this the first time you've been here at the Retreat?'

'No, this will be the third time.'

This was interesting. Luca had asked the manager for a list of all guests who had been here before but I hadn't seen it. Although mentally I had been tending to rule out people well known to the club, it occurred to me that if these two had been here the previous year at the same time as Joseph Beck, something might have happened that was now carrying on into this year.

As far as the night of the first murder was concerned, Muller told us he and his wife had driven down to the coast, where they had had a late dinner and then gone to a nightclub until well past midnight. He provided the name of the club and the inspector instructed Sergeant Rossi to check if there might be CCTV footage to confirm the alibi. However, as far as Wednesday night when Griffiths had been killed was concerned, Muller claimed that he and his wife had spent it alone and nobody could vouch for them.

The inspector and I fired more questions at him without receiving any significant answers, although by this time, the sweat was pouring off Muller's chest in cascades. Finally, I changed the direction of our questioning.

'I was interested to see that this is a no-children resort. There seem to be a lot of good-looking couples here and I've been wondering what brings them here. Do they come just for a holiday or is there more to it than that? Could this be a place where couples hook up with other like-minded couples? There's a word in English that we use and that's "swingers". Have you heard it before?' This thought had been occurring to me on and off since I had got here, although I hadn't observed anything untoward going on. I thought it worth querying but I was unprepared for the effect my question had on the German.

He jumped as if he'd been stung and the inspector and I exchanged looks. Muller did his best to reply but he had to clear his throat nervously first. 'We use the same word in German.'

'Is that why you come here? Are you and your wife swingers?' He was now so red in the face I was genuinely concerned for his well-being so I added a bit of reassurance. 'This is a murder inquiry, Mr Muller, so we have to ask these questions. Anything you tell us which doesn't impact the investigation will remain strictly between us, is that clear? Now, I'll ask you again, do you and your wife come here for that reason? Like I say, it's completely up to you how you live your lives and we aren't here to judge. What we're trying to do is to find a killer.'

I deliberately added a bit of extra emphasis to the final word and then let it hang in the air. After probably only ten seconds but what felt like a minute or two, Muller looked up from his hands and nodded.

'Yes.' He took a couple of deep breaths. 'But if word of it should ever get back to Frankfurt, it could destroy me. I have a lot of elderly and very old-fashioned people who come to me with their animals. I'm sure such a revelation could ruin my reputation and potentially close down my veterinary practice.' He looked up with an anguished expression on his face. 'But, even worse, I'm a respected member of the city council and a scandal like this could spoil not only my chances of re-election but those of the whole party. Please don't let a word of this leak out, I beg you.'

'In the light of this admission, would you like to rethink your statement that you and your wife were alone on Wednesday night?' The inspector had adopted a sympathetic tone. 'Establishing an alibi would be helpful to you.'

Muller shook his head. 'I wish I could, but no, we were all alone.'

The swinging thing and his fear for his reputation explained why he and his wife had been so nervous. The question remained, however, whether this was the sole cause of their anxiety or whether a darker secret might lie below the surface.

After he'd left the room, I looked across at Luca. 'Now that was interesting, wasn't it? I wonder who else is here for the same reason. Maybe that's why the Hungarian couple appeared nervous and, indeed, why the Smith couple have been arguing. Maybe she objected to what he was proposing.'

The inspector nodded. 'Or the other way round. You might well be right and, of course, if there has been a lot of sexual impropriety taking place, that increases the likelihood that our murders were crimes of passion – or lust.'

16

FRIDAY LATE MORNING

This completed the interviews with guests on our shortlist and we were left with the two potentially suspicious staff members. We started with the man at the gate, Dario Dolcedo. Interestingly, when he came in wearing his usual polo shirt and shorts, I was momentarily taken aback. I'd got so used to seeing naked people by now – apart from the police – that the sight of somebody wearing clothes appeared almost bizarre. He confirmed that he and his wife, Rita, had worked here for some years and had been here the previous summer when Joseph Beck had also been a guest. Once again, when pressed about his knowledge of any possible liaison between his wife and Joseph Beck, he shook his head and appeared to get quite annoyed.

'Rita and I love each other. She would never be unfaithful to me and I would never be unfaithful to her. I don't know what kind of dirty world you policemen live in, but don't include us in your smutty thoughts.' As he spoke, I couldn't miss the gold crucifix on a thin chain around his neck. Maybe noticing the direction of my eyes, he reached for the cross and held it out towards us. 'We're both regular churchgoers and we know the difference between right and wrong. Rita is pure and so am I, and I deeply resent your implications.'

Luca poured a bit of oil on troubled waters by giving him the standard explanation that in a murder investigation, we had no option but to ask awkward questions and that no slight had been intended. Dario grudgingly accepted his justification and repeated his and his wife's innocence of any kind of extramarital hanky-panky, but also of any possible thought of murder.

When he had left the room, I glanced across at Luca.

'He sounded pretty convincing.'

Luca didn't look quite so sure. 'I don't know. In my experience, guilty suspects often try to adopt the moral high ground, so I wouldn't rule him out yet. I thought the crucifix was a little bit too theatrical.' He looked across at the sergeant. 'Right, Rossi, let's see what the wife has to say for herself.'

Just like her husband, Rita denied any kind of romantic association with Joseph Beck either this year or the previous year. When we told her that several people had commented on the fact that she and the Englishman had been seen together, she didn't deny it. 'Yes, of course people would have seen us together. He was a regular in the gym every morning and every evening and, inevitably, we talked quite a bit. I liked him and I did spend quite a bit of time with him, but that's as far as it went. I love my husband and my marriage vows mean something to me... unlike a lot of people here at this place.' That was distinct disapproval in her voice, so I did a bit of digging.

'We've heard that some of the guests come here to have sex with other couples. Is that what you mean?'

She nodded. 'That's exactly what I mean. It's disgusting.'

'Surely, how people live their lives is up to them. What gives us the right to judge?'

Her expression turned to one of revulsion. 'It's obscene, it's degrading and it's against the will of God.' She, too, was wearing a golden crucifix and she made the sign of the cross with her fingers above it. 'Dario and I think it's disgusting.'

'So why do you keep working here?'

'Jobs aren't so easy to find these days. Besides, there aren't many naturist camps in Italy and I love the fact that here is somewhere I can be as the good Lord intended, naked and innocent just like the Garden of Eden.'

I saw the sergeant over by the door roll his eyes and I picked up on her biblical reference. 'Until the snake comes along. It would appear that Joseph Beck didn't share your moral scruples. How could you be friends with a person like that?'

'I only found out very recently what kind of man he was.' She looked up and I could see the anger on her face. 'First it was Leo's daughter and now it's that model girl. All he could think about was sex. It's obscene.'

'Did you say Leo's daughter?' This came as a bolt from the blue. Well, I reflected, maybe not entirely. All along, I'd had the feeling that Bianca Moretti hadn't been 100 per cent open with me, but what did this mean to the investigation? I bottled up the host of ideas racing through my head for now and double-checked what Rita had just said. 'You mean Bianca? Was she having an affair with Joseph Beck?'

A more apprehensive look appeared on her face. 'Of course, you're friends with Leo, aren't you? Yes, I'm sure she was, but you didn't hear that from me, all right? Like I say, jobs are hard to find.'

'I presume you know her quite well? Did Bianca ever mention Joseph Beck to you?'

'Not a word, but I saw them together and I just knew there was something going on.'

'Do you think that something was going on last year or only more recently?'

'They were both here last year and I've certainly seen them together this year, but she's been away on and off over the last week or two.' She caught my eye and she was positively glowering. 'And that's why he got himself the model. And they're not the only ones, I'm sure. It's disgusting...'

She was unable or unwilling to provide any concrete proof or even names of any other sexual partners Beck might have had, but one thing was clear: her feelings for the first victim had been very different from what we had imagined. She hadn't loved him, she had loathed him.

Or had she?

After she'd gone off, I did my best to explain to Luca what this new information about Bianca might do to the investigation if it turned out to be true. I had already told him briefly how it was that I'd come here to the Retreat but I went into more detail and, in particular, I mentioned my doubts as to the veracity of what Bianca had told me during our meeting back in Florence.

'When I first arrested her just over two years ago, it very quickly emerged that she wasn't going to cooperate. She's an intelligent woman and it was clear that she was only telling us the bare minimum. When I saw her in Florence on Monday, I got the impression – well, more of a hunch, really – that she knew more than she was letting on, but I certainly didn't expect this. I presume she comes over here every summer to stay with her father, so if she was joining in with the fun here at the Retreat, it's no surprise that she met Beck. But if she did, why didn't she mention it to me? What we need to work out is how serious her relationship with him was and whether it might have gone sour enough to provoke her to murder.' Although deep down, I found it hard to imagine her as a killer, I reflected that she wouldn't be the first suspect to manage to completely bamboozle a detective.

Luca looked as puzzled as I was feeling. 'But if you're saying that things might have gone sour between them to the extent that she decided to kill him, then why on earth did she get *you* involved? As you know, as far as we were concerned, the first death was an accident so why would she want to stir that up?'

I nodded in agreement. 'I know what you mean; it makes no sense.' An unsettling thought occurred to me. 'Maybe she deliberately chose to come to me because she felt I was incompetent enough not to get to the truth.' I saw Luca grin but he said nothing. I gave a frustrated snort that made Oscar raise his nose from the floor and shoot me a concerned look. I leant down and ruffled his ears as I continued. 'One thing's for sure: we need to sit down and have a long talk to Bianca Moretti. She told me she's coming back today. There's more to this than meets the eye.'

Luca stood up and looked at his watch. 'It's gone twelve o'clock and I'm getting hungry. There's an excellent pizzeria down near the beach.' He glanced down at me. 'Feel like joining us? They have tables outside, so you can bring your dog.'

We drove down together with the sergeant in the police Alfa. Guests at the Pizzeria da Tonino were treated to the unusual spectacle of a squad car pulling up in the car park with three men and a dog in it. The owner clearly knew Luca and he showed us to a table right at the far end of the terrace where we could talk without being overheard. The pizzeria was situated alongside the church, and the terrace was just above the roofs of the houses down at sea level below. From here, the view across the bay and along the sandy beach with its parallel lines of brightly coloured parasols was archetypically Italian and there was a definite holiday vibe in the air. It felt almost improper to be discussing two brutal murders but we knew that that was what we had to do.

After we had ordered three of the house special pizzas, and the waiter had brought us bottles of water and white wine, Luca made a start.

'So, who do we have? First things first: are we convinced that both murders were the work of the same perpetrator and the second victim almost certainly killed to stop him talking?' Rossi and I nodded in unison and he continued, counting on his fingers. 'Right, we have Rita and Dario Dolcedo. They both insist there was nothing going on between the wife and Beck, but that contradicts what a couple of witnesses have said. How about this as a scenario? Rita and Beck are having a relationship, the husband finds out and kills Beck. Alternatively, Rita was having a relationship but when she discovers that Beck was carrying on with Bianca Moretti and Kim Russell, she flips and takes her revenge.' He looked across the table at the two of us. 'What do you think?'

Rossi answered first. 'I don't know about you two, but I tended to believe her when she said there was nothing going on between her and Beck. If so, then no jealousy and no murder.' He gave me an interrogative glance. 'What do you think... Dan?'

'I tended to believe her as well, but what *we* believe and what her husband believed are two different things. Maybe she really didn't have an affair, but her husband convinced himself she did. As a result, he killed Beck in revenge for something that never happened. As for the others, I got the impression Kim Russell was telling the truth and that her relationship with the first victim might have been little more than friendship. Certainly, I couldn't sense the sort of intense passion that can lead to murder. Her girlfriend, Melinda, on the other hand, looks like a tougher character altogether and jealousy can be a powerful motivator.'

Luca nodded and continued, still counting on his fingers. 'So Dario Dolcedo and Melinda Barker, that's two possibles. What about the Mullers? The husband has told us that he and his wife were swingers and everybody says Beck was sexually promiscuous so might he have been the third wheel in their relationship? Might the husband have killed him in a fit of jealous rage?'

The sergeant answered. 'Or was Beck blackmailing them, threatening to spread the word around Frankfurt that they were swingers and they killed him to shut him up?'

I wasn't totally convinced by either argument so I just shrugged my shoulders and Luca carried on. 'Okay, that's three and we'll keep him on the list for now. How about Schinken, the other German? He's old enough to have been active at the time when Beck was shot. Might he have killed Beck to prevent himself from being denounced as the person who betrayed Beck and his mother?'

I had given them an edited summary of Beck's story and I'd been doing a lot of thinking about the likelihood of the murder having a link to the past. A thought occurred to me and I picked up my phone. 'I've never been great at geography. I just want to check something.'

I pulled up a map of Germany, on which I quickly found Chemnitz. As I had suspected, Dresden, the home of Klaus Schinken, was little more than forty or fifty miles away from there. As I was studying the map, my eyes flicked down an inch into the Czech Republic and I noticed that just over the border was none other than Karlovy Vary, a similar short distance from Chemnitz. I looked up again at the two police officers and pushed my phone across the table towards them.

'If we're looking for a link with Beck's home town, both Schinken and Adam Novotny live close by. That's quite a coincidence, and I don't like coincidences.'

Conversation was temporarily interrupted by the arrival of

three huge pizzas. It came as no surprise so close to the fishing port to see that the house specials were smothered in seafood. The mix of prawns, octopus pieces and squid rings with wonderful, melted cheese was excellent and I made a mental note to bring Anna here in two weeks' time – assuming, of course, that she agreed to come with me after my faux pas the other day.

While we were eating, I searched my phone for more information on Karlovy Vary and discovered something interesting. The important spa town had originally been called Karlsbad and it had been part of the Sudetenland, a German-speaking area within the borders of the former Czechoslovakia. In 1938, the area was annexed by Germany and the very next year, Adolf Hitler sent his troops into Poland, setting in motion a chain of events that led to the outbreak of war and the suffering of millions. At the end of the war, the area was returned to Czechoslovakia and many German speakers fled back across the border or were forcibly ejected. Maybe Novotny's family had German roots and closer links to Chemnitz or even the Stasi than I had first thought.

I translated the article to the two officers while we were eating and they both took notes. We were approaching the end of the meal when Luca brought the conversation back to the double murders. 'The German connection is definitely worth following up. Rossi, get onto our German colleagues and ask them to give Klaus Schinken an in-depth check, particularly looking for any links to the security services or the Stasi. How long has he been a shopkeeper? What sort of shop is it? What did he do before that? Where was he in 1987? As for Novotny, he would have been little more than a child when Beck escaped from East Germany but ask the Czechs to look into not only him but his parents as well. You never know.'

I nodded approvingly and looked across at the sergeant. 'What about the report on the British people? Has it arrived yet?'

'Yes and no. I've just had a message a moment or two ago to say that a partial report has arrived. They've sent the reports on Mr and Mrs Harcourt, Melinda Barker and Kim Russell, but not the other two. The email with it apologises for the delay and says that they're having trouble collecting full information on Jeremy Smith.'

Luca and I exchanged glances and he reacted first. 'I wonder what that means. Could it be that Smith was also something to do with the security services or is there more to it than that? Either way, I think that confirms the feeling we all got about him. I definitely got the impression that neither he nor his lady friend were telling us the whole truth. Let's hope they get that information to us soon. I look forward to reading the details. Dan, maybe you'd be so kind as to go through the report on the Harcourt couple and Barker and Russell once we've finished eating?' He picked up his glass and took a mouthful. 'Anyway, apart from the British contingent, how do we feel about the Hungarian couple? Might there be a connection there with Beck's past? After all, Hungary was also a part of the Soviet empire back then.'

It was an interesting thought but none of us could come up with a connection between Mr and Mrs Farkas and either of the dead men apart, possibly, from something linked to the obvious bed-hopping that had been going on in the camp. I thought back to the MI6 man's final words. There could be no doubt that the first victim had been an inveterate womaniser and particularly in a sexually charged environment like this, it was easy to see how emotions – or at least lust – could run high. Had Beck been murdered by a jealous husband or boyfriend like Dario Dolcedo or even a jealous girlfriend in the shape of Melinda Barker? Alternatively, had he been murdered by a woman scorned like Rita Dolcedo, Kim Russell or even Bianca? One thing was for sure: as soon as Bianca returned later today from wherever she'd been, I wanted to sit down and have a long hard talk to Ms Moretti.

I demolished the last of my pizza – well, to be honest, not exactly the last. Oscar and I have a deal that he always gets a piece of crust right at the end. I took a big mouthful of cold, white wine and followed it with half a glass of mineral water before reaching across the table to pick up the sergeant's phone. The report from the UK police on Oliver and Fleur Harcourt was fairly minimal. No convictions, nothing untoward, they appeared to be completely on the level. They were described as retired and their address was given as Orchard House, Little Ducklington. It definitely sounded right but something was still nagging me, but maybe that was just my suspicious nature. Just then, something occurred to me and I pulled out my phone.

I remembered the red and blue tattoo on Harcourt's forearm and I googled 'Grenadier Guards' to find that his tattoo exactly matched the insignia of the regiment, right down to the *Honi Soit Qui Mal y Pense* – Evil be to him who thinks evil – wording around the sides. Out of interest, I also checked the parachute wings insignia I had spotted on his other arm and was slightly surprised to see that this was normally just that: a pair of wings. I couldn't remember exactly but I felt sure I had spotted something on top of Harcourt's wings. A word? A logo? An image? Maybe it would prove to be irrelevant but I resolved to take a closer look next time I saw him just in case.

The report on Melinda and Kim, on the other hand, made fascinating reading.

Melinda Barker was described as a very successful business-woman. She had been married briefly fifteen years previously but had divorced almost immediately. Interestingly, the divorce had been filed by the husband on the grounds of physical and verbal abuse. Clearly this indicated that underneath the love and peace exterior, Melinda definitely had a tougher side and, at least fifteen years previously, an interest in men. Might that indicate that she had indeed been attracted to Beck and, when he'd spurned her advances, she had killed him? Alternatively, might she have killed him when he took an interest in her girlfriend, Kim?

Kim Russell had a caution for Class A drugs use but not dealing, without any further action having been taken. Otherwise, apart from three points on her licence for speeding in a built-up area, her record was clean. The person who had compiled the report had added a fascinating note at the bottom indicating that there was currently a lot of media speculation about her and an American actor called Nick Pool. Apparently they had been seen together and he had been spotted recently shopping for rings at Tiffanys in New York. It was clear that any feelings she might have for Melinda were far from exclusive.

I gave the two officers a quick translation of the reports and Luca thanked me. The three of us agreed that Mr and Mrs Harcourt were unlikely to have been our killers, although I made a mental note to ask Paul in London to dig a little deeper into this seemingly classic English couple. Maybe it was just good old-fashioned prejudice on my part, but I needed to be sure they weren't too good to be true.

Luca swallowed his espresso and the three of us stood up. 'Hopefully, in the course of this afternoon, we'll hear from the UK about Mr Smith and his friend, and from the German and Czech authorities about the others. As soon as Bianca Moretti surfaces, Dan, will you give me a call?' He glanced at his watch. 'Two o'clock. Rossi, would you drop Dan back up to the Retreat? I think I'll walk back to the station to clear my head. It's been a long morning.'

17

FRIDAY AFTERNOON

I got back to the tower just in time to see Leo coming out of the gates in the pickup. He stopped to tell me he was popping out to go shopping and to help myself to anything I wanted. Without trying to sound too interested, I asked him when he was expecting Bianca to return and he told me she'd been delayed but should be here by four or five o'clock. As the gates closed behind him, and Oscar and I walked up the drive to the tower, I pulled out my phone. While Oscar proceeded to mark what he now considered to be his territory, I took a seat on a convenient bench in the shade and called London. The phone was answered by one of Paul's colleagues called DC Seymour who told me that he was in a meeting. I asked her if she would mind giving him a message. I passed on what details I had of Mr and Mrs Harcourt and asked if he could possibly do a bit of digging. She must have recognised my name although I didn't recognise hers and she very kindly offered to check them out herself. I thanked her warmly and rang off.

I sat there, holding the phone in my hands, knowing that I

was facing a dilemma in my personal life that was as thorny a subject as the twin murders here at the Retreat.

I had told Anna that I would be back tonight and, if I was going to do that, I knew I would have to leave here by five o'clock if I didn't want to arrive home in the dead of night. I was torn. Part of me knew that the sooner I got back to see her, the sooner we could talk about Tuesday night and hopefully resolve things between us. The problem was that another part of me wanted to stay, at least until we had all the information on our potential suspects. The idea of leaving a murder investigation partway through – even though it wasn't strictly my investigation – was anathema to me. I sat there in the shade of the umbrella pine for quite some time before coming to a decision that wouldn't have surprised my ex-wife.

I took the coward's way out and sent Anna a text message rather than calling her, simply saying that I had been delayed and hoping we could meet up tomorrow. It was a cop out, but I suppose I knew deep down that telling her the truth about why I was choosing to stay on might well have sounded the death knell of our relationship.

The deed done, I opened the front door and Oscar and I walked into the wonderfully cool interior of the tower. Upstairs, I gave him his delayed lunch, made myself a cup of tea, and then sat down to have a think. Shelving my own personal dilemma for now, I concentrated on our possible suspects. Dario Dolcedo was definitely a contender and the German connection was compelling – whether Schinken, Muller or even Novotny. Could there really be a link with events on the German border all those years ago? Jeremy Smith looked like a bad lot and his girlfriend questionable. Hopefully, when the reports on them came through, we would know more. Melinda Barker committing a crime of passion, or at least jealousy, also had to remain in the frame. I couldn't see Kim, the beautiful model, as a killer and I ignored her for now so, unless Paul could come up with something juicy on Mr and Mrs Harcourt, this gave us seven suspects we had already interviewed, but now there was an eighth: Bianca.

As I had the house to myself, I left Oscar stretched out on the kitchen floor, strategically positioned between the fridge and the hob, and went up to the next floor where Leo had told me Bianca's room was situated. I knew this to be right opposite the one I was currently occupying, so I tapped on the door just in case Bianca had returned unbeknown to her father and, getting no reply, I opened it and glanced around. I wasn't really sure what I was looking for but I got a surprise all the same. Somehow I had been expecting to see somewhere full of personal stuff, clothes, jewellery maybe, possibly even a photo or two, but the room was as bleak and empty as a hotel room. There was a big king-size bed just like the one in my room and there wasn't a wrinkle in the crisp, white cover, again just like a hotel room. Did this mean she hadn't been staying here after all?

I stepped inside and took a closer look. A quick check in the chest of drawers did at least produce some results. I found a couple of immaculately folded jumpers, a fleece, socks and underwear. In the walk-in wardrobe, half a dozen blouses and dresses were hanging from a rail with another handful of tops and shorts and bits and pieces on the shelves alongside but, considering this was her father's house and she presumably returned here time after time, there was very little. On the floor were a pair of flip-flops not dissimilar to the ones I had just bought and a single pair of sandals. In fact, she could probably have got everything in this room into one not oversized suitcase. A quick glance in the bathroom revealed it to be almost completely empty but presumably she had taken her bits and pieces with her wherever she had gone over the past couple of days, along with at least some more clothes. Even so, the place looked more like the *Mary Celeste* than a woman's bedroom.

I returned to the bedroom door and took one last look around. What struck me most of all was the total lack of anything personal, not even a crumpled tissue or an old boarding pass. I found myself wondering whether she maybe suffered from some sort of obsessive compulsive disorder or whether she'd given up on intimate personal belongings during her time in prison. I knew from talking to other former prisoners that the stark emptiness of a prison cell could have a seriously depressing effect on people, and for a moment I felt guilty that I had been the person responsible for inflicting that on her. Doing my best to remind myself that she had brought that upon herself, I carefully closed the door and went back downstairs again.

Oscar raised his head when he heard me come down the steps but then lowered it back to the floor again with a sigh. I sat down on one of the sofas and considered what I should do next. As soon as Bianca returned, she was top priority but, in the meantime, I wondered if there might be anything to be gained from taking another look around the Retreat. I glanced through one of the small windows at the sunlit scene outside. One of the disadvantages of living in a medieval fortress was that the original builders deliberately made the windows too narrow for marauding hordes to squeeze through – particularly windows within easy climbing distance of the ground – so the views were somewhat limited. The upside to this, coupled with the fact that the walls were at least a metre thick, was that although the temperature outside was well into the thirties, in here without any aircon, the temperature was perfect. Oscar had even stopped panting. Being a black dog in hot sunshine can't be a lot of fun even if you were born over here, as he was.

A glance at my watch told me that I had ample time to take one more look at the Retreat before Bianca's return so I summoned my canine companion and headed off in that direction, taking a brief detour through the scrub for Oscar to stretch his legs first, but it was far too hot for a serious walk and even he didn't look particularly enthusiastic. The prospect of a refreshing swim for both of us had distinct appeal and I was soon back in the changing room. By now, it felt almost natural to strip off, don solely my flip-flops, pick up my replacement plastic bag with my wallet, phone and notebook, and walk along the path through the rosemary bushes. The volleyball aficionados had very sensibly decided against running around in this heat and I saw that most people had gravitated towards the pool. Oscar's eyes lit up as he saw the water and he ran the last few yards and leapt in with a spectacular belly flop that sent a plume of spray into the air and earned a round of applause from amused spectators.

I left my things on a convenient bench and joined him in the water – in less spectacular fashion – and swam around gratefully. To my surprise, a few minutes later, as I was treading water and minding my own business, I heard a voice at my ear.

'Could I have a word, Officer?'

I turned my head to find none other than Kim the model swimming towards me. As ever, she looked worried.

'Not an officer any longer, Kim. I'm just Dan nowadays.'

'But you're working with the police, right?'

I deliberately played down my involvement. 'I'm just giving them a bit of help with interpreting.' I paddled around until I was facing her and made sure Oscar kept a safe distance in case he tried to repeat his favourite swimming-pool trick by climbing on Kim's shoulders. 'How can I help?'

I saw her cast a wary eye all around, but we were in a relatively quiet spot and she could see that we wouldn't be overheard. Even so, she lowered her voice. 'I feel I should explain myself. I'm here with Melinda but the fact is that I have a boyfriend.'

I wondered if this was the American actor mentioned in the UK police report, but for now, I just gave her an interrogative look. 'A man who's here now? Somebody who was here before, like Joseph Beck for example?'

She shook her head violently. 'No, absolutely not. I already told you about him. Yes, I liked him but that's as far as it went. No, this is another guy. I've been seeing him for quite a few months now and things have got serious; in fact, so serious that we're about to take it to the next level. Of course, he knows I'm here with Melinda, but hopefully nobody else does. I was just wondering if you could maybe have a word with that police inspector to ask him if he could please make sure news of my presence here with her doesn't leak out. I'm quite a well-known face these days and my guy's even more famous, and I'm terrified people might jump to the wrong conclusion and embarrass both of us.'

'The wrong conclusion? About what?'

'It's not what you think.' I almost smiled to hear her repeat Leo Moretti's words but I gave no response and waited for her to explain. I didn't have long to wait. 'Two women together, she's sort of my boss and it would be natural for me to want to keep her sweet, so, you know... People can think what they like but there's nothing going on. I mean, nothing sexual. I know there's a lot of bed-hopping going on at this place but I'm not involved and Melinda's not involved and she and I are just good friends. I mean that.' Her expression became more helpless, more pleading. 'But you can see how people might put two and two together and get five, can't you?'

I certainly could. That was exactly the conclusion I'd come to. 'I see.' I chose my words carefully. 'You're right, I can easily see how people might misconstrue your relationship. Of course I'll speak to the inspector. Unless you or Melinda turn out to be a murderer, I'm sure your name won't be made public. Please tell me neither of you are murderers.'

She looked genuinely horrified. 'Good God, no.'

'Not you, not Melinda?'

'Absolutely not.'

I had already mentally discounted Kim as a murder suspect, but this news about the platonic nature of her relationship with Melinda – assuming it wasn't a smokescreen – was potentially of considerable interest. Our scenario of Melinda killing Beck in a moment of jealous rage was looking less likely. Seeing as I had Kim in communicative mode, I tried a question.

'You said you were friendly with Beck. Did he ever speak to you about his life, his job, whether there was a special person in his life? Anything at all really? We know so little about him.'

I saw her pause for thought. 'Hardly anything, to be honest. He was one of those people who was great at getting other people to talk. For a man, he was a remarkably good listener, but he didn't give much away.'

I did my best to jog her memory. 'Did he tell you why he chose to come here? Was it a recommendation from a friend or do you think he was deeply into the whole naturist thing?'

'He told me he came here last year and it was his first experience of naturism, but he enjoyed it so much, that's why he came back.'

'And who do you think recommended it to him in the first place?'

'I really don't know.'

'Apart from you, do you think he was close to anybody else here?'

'I think he was quite friendly with a woman called Bianca. I haven't seen her for a couple of days but she was here all last week and although they didn't seem to spend much time together, I definitely got the feeling they knew each other.' She smiled. 'I can tell you this. If I wasn't in a strong relationship already, I could have fancied him a lot, and there was just something about the way he looked at Bianca that made me feel almost jealous.'

After she had swum off, I floated around for another few minutes, reflecting on what she had told me about Bianca and Joseph Beck. Could it really be that they had been in some sort of relationship? And if they had been, could Bianca have had anything to do with his death? It made little sense. If she had murdered him for whatever reason, why, as Luca had said, had she then got me involved? All she had to do would have been to let sleeping dogs lie and that would have been the end of it. Alternatively, had she got me involved because she thought she knew the identity of the killer but she needed my expertise to prove it? But, if that were the case, why hadn't she said anything to the police last weekend and why hadn't she told me of her suspicions?

I swam slowly down to the far end of the pool with a happy Labrador beside me and, as I did so, a thought occurred to me. If Bianca had been in some sort of relationship with Beck that nobody here at the Retreat had noticed, apart from a few occasional glances or brief exchanges, how and where might this relationship have been carried out? The answer wasn't hard to find. I remembered Leo's slight hesitation on the occasions when I had asked him if Bianca and Beck had known each other. Had they carried out their tryst in Leo's tower? I now knew that I needed to speak to Leo again as well as his daughter but, first, I needed to speak to the manager of the Retreat.

I retrieved my flip-flops and we made our way up to the bar. Although it barely took a couple of minutes to get there, the baking heat and the bright sunshine had almost completely dried me off by the time I arrived. I sat down at my usual table against the wall of the clubhouse and Oscar at my feet, rolling around on his back on the tiled floor, grunting and growling happily to himself. Less than a minute later, Sophie appeared.

'*Ciao*, Dan, how's the investigation going? Any closer to knowing who did it?'

I shrugged my shoulders. 'You'd better ask the inspector. I think it's fair to say he's narrowed it down to just a few suspects but as far as I know, he's still looking for a motive and for definite proof.' I gave her a little smile. 'Don't worry, your name isn't on the list.'

I saw her shudder. 'Perish the thought. I just hope you manage to catch the killer sooner rather than later because the atmosphere here today has been dire.' Remembering her job description, she did her best to return my smile. 'Anyway, you look like you could do with a cold beer and I'm sure Oscar's thirsty as well.'

'You took the words right out of my mouth. Oh, and by the way, is George about?'

'I'll check in his office and he'll come out to see you.'

Two minutes later, George himself came out carrying a bowl of water and a bottle of ice-cold beer. 'Hi, Dan. Sophie said you wanted a word.'

He set the drinks down and I explained what I wanted. 'You told me that the bracelets we all wear register on the computer every time we open the pedestrian gate. That's right, isn't it?' He nodded so I continued. 'I wonder if you could check something for me. Would it be possible to let me know Joseph Beck's movements every day last week until his death? I'd like to know whether he spent all his time here at the camp or whether he went out at all.'

'Of course, I'll get onto it now and I'll get Sophie to bring you a printout in a few minutes.'

18

FRIDAY AFTERNOON

Armed with the printout, I went back to the tower at just after three to find Leo's pickup parked there once more. I was about to go inside to confront him when my phone started ringing. It was Sergeant Rossi.

'The inspector's got the reports back from Germany and from England. He asks if you could spare the time to come down and go through them with him. He says they look interesting. I can come and pick you up if you like.'

I didn't hesitate. 'Of course I'll come. Thanks for the offer but I'll drive down with Oscar.' I knew I wanted to speak to Leo but that would have to wait. I was genuinely keen to read what the UK police said about Jeremy Smith and Lorraine Hickson so I told Rossi I would come straight away.

On the way down the hill, I almost had an accident as a motorbike came hurtling up around a blind corner and nearly wiped both of us out and I noticed a long, green scrape along the stone wall on the corner where a previous driver hadn't been so lucky. Since arriving in Italy two years earlier, I had been pleasantly surprised to find that Italian drivers – in spite of a reputation for thoughtlessness – were not that different from their UK counterparts. Most people behave sensibly, but there are morons everywhere.

I parked close to the *questura* and went in to find Luca with a couple of sheets of paper in his hands. '*Ciao*, Dan. Take a look at this. It makes interesting reading.'

I scanned quickly through the first, fairly long paragraph and then gave him a translation in case he'd missed anything.

'Jeremy Peter Smith, known to most people as Jezza, comes from Catford, South London. Left school at age sixteen with no qualifications. Worked for two years in a local café and, from there, moved up in the hospitality business, first working in pubs and then discos and nightclubs. Currently manager of the Green Parrot in Lewisham, a strip club rumoured to be a front for a brothel. Spent two years in Belmarsh prison in the early 2000s for handling stolen property and supplying Class A drugs and another three years in Brixton jail from 2008 to 2011 for more drug-related stuff and GBH – that's grievous bodily harm. He and another man were found guilty of beating a Jamaican national so badly, the man spent three weeks in hospital. No convictions since then, but a number of warnings for drunkenness and abusive behaviour. Currently a person of interest in an ongoing drug investigation.' I looked up at the two officers. 'Not a very nice man.'

'The ongoing drug investigation sounds interesting, given that you were told that Joseph Beck had been investigating that sort of thing.' Luca shot me an interrogative look. 'Any chance you could ask your friend at Scotland Yard to look into that a bit more deeply? If you go direct, it might speed things up.'

I nodded. 'Definitely. I'll give him a call. I wonder why it took them so long to send us this. They said something about him being hard to locate, didn't they?'

'Maybe this ongoing drug investigation held things up. Don't worry about it. Check out what it says about his girlfriend Lorraine Hickson.'

I let my eye run on down the page.

'The report on Jeremy Smith doesn't mention a wife or girl-friend and the report on Lorraine Hickson mentions nothing either, so if they are in a relationship, it's either pretty recent or it's very low-key.'

'Or it's fictitious.' His tone was dry.

I nodded. 'Indeed. The report on Lorraine just confirms pretty much what we've suspected. She works as a stripper but has been picked up and cautioned by the vice squad on two occasions on suspicion of prostitution. No actual convictions, though. How's this for a scenario? Jeremy "Jezza" Smith is sent over here to silence Beck, who's been getting too nosey for the bosses of the drug ring. To give him extra cover and a useful female decoy, he brings a hooker with him to look like his partner. Does that sound credible?'

They both nodded and the inspector replied. 'Yes, indeed and, conveniently, the couple were sitting close to Owen Griffiths when he said that thing to the waitress about being sure it was murder. I think it's safe to assume that Griffiths saw or heard something relating to Beck's murder and was eliminated before he could tell us. I think this raises Smith to the top of the list for now but, unless we find DNA evidence that points to him, we're still short of enough proof to nail him.'

I nodded but the sergeant still wasn't giving up on the possi-bility of the murder having been a crime of passion. 'Why would Smith go to all the trouble of coming over here to kill Beck when both he and the victim were in London only a couple of weeks ago? I still think Beck might have been murdered by one of the other people here for a completely different reason – the jealous husband of the fitness instructor, for example.'

I passed on what I had just heard from Kim and saw comprehension dawn on the faces of the two detectives. 'We still need to check, but this certainly makes our scenario of the jealous lesbian lover less likely, but it also potentially brings Bianca Moretti into the frame.'

'You think she killed Beck?' Sergeant Rossi sounded surprised.

I shook my head in bemusement. 'I honestly don't know. She's a tough character but I didn't think her capable of murder two years ago and I still find it hard to believe now. The thing is, I would bet good money that she and Beck were in a relationship. They were very circumspect – for whatever reason – but this printout of the gate opening times shows that Joseph Beck left the Retreat almost every night last week at around half past eleven and returned next morning before the maintenance man arrived at six-thirty. Any guesses where he spent the night?'

To my surprise, Luca appeared almost annoyed to receive this information. He was quick to explain. 'Damn, that means we now have to consider Bianca Moretti as a potential suspect as well, although why she would kill the man she was sleeping with remains to be seen. The thing is, if we relegate the English-woman, Melinda Barker, to the ranks of possibles rather than probables, we were heading for a three-horse race: Jeremy Smith, Dario Dolcedo or Klaus Schinken.' Seeing the quizzical expression on my face, he nodded. 'We've just received further information about the Czech and German suspects. Nothing incriminating to report on Adam Novotny, but something very interesting indeed has emerged about Herr Schinken. Here...' He handed me another sheet of paper. 'Take a look.'

The information was indeed fascinating. Klaus Schinken

currently ran a gun shop in a town called Freital, ten kilometres from Dresden in Saxony. It appeared that he had taken over the shop originally owned by his father, Wilhelm, in 1988. This wasn't the interesting part of the report. What really leapt off the pages was the fact that he had previously been an employee of East Germany's Ministry for State Security, AKA the Stasi. Lacking a university degree, he had become a non-commissioned officer and this lowly rank had probably saved him from in-depth investigation during the years after the fall of the Soviet Union. Presumably, he had seen the writing on the wall – literally as well as figuratively – and had left the Stasi just before the dissolution of the hated organisation and the subsequent recriminations.

I handed the sheet back to Luca and exhaled. 'Wow! I see what you mean. This could potentially be extremely interesting.'

Luca took the report back and dropped it on his desk. He picked up his pen and wrote four names on a blank sheet of paper:

Dolcedo
Smith
Schinken
Moretti

He tapped the paper with his finger. 'Are we happy to exclude Melinda Barker for now? We'll keep her in mind, but I think these four are more likely.' We both nodded so he sat back and looked at us. 'Well, take your pick, gentlemen.'

I thought about it for a few moments and then suggested another name. 'It probably means nothing, but I've asked my friend Paul at Scotland Yard to check out Mr and Mrs Harcourt. They may turn out to be totally innocent but there was just something about them that didn't ring true.'

The inspector added the word 'Harcourt' to the list and then looked across at the two of us.

'Tomorrow's Saturday and its departure day for both Smith and Schinken and...' he consulted another printout '...and the Harcourts leave tomorrow as well. Dolcedo and Moretti will presumably still be staying on, but if the killer is one of the others, we only have a few hours to come up with enough proof to hold them. Any ideas?'

I spoke first. 'As I see it, there are two things I need to do and I'll get onto them straight away. I'll phone London to see if my contacts there have come up with anything new on Mr and Mrs Harcourt. If those two get a clean bill of health, at least we can remove them from the list. While I'm at it, I'll also ask Paul if he can make a few calls to find out more about Smith's involvement in the drug investigation that's mentioned.'

Luca gave a grunt of agreement. 'Thank you, Dan. That'll be a big help. It's clear that we need to interview Bianca Moretti as a matter of urgency; when did her father say she'd be back?'

I glanced at my watch. 'Any minute now. She should have been back earlier but he said she'd been delayed. Rather than have you waste your time, why don't I go back to the tower now and I'll call you just as soon as she returns from wherever she's been? Besides, I'd like to sit down with her father first. I have a feeling he knows more than he's letting on. Whether or not I can get anything out of him remains to be seen but I think it's worth a try.'

19

FRIDAY AFTERNOON

As soon as I got outside, I stood on the pavement in the shade of a convenient tree and called Scotland Yard. The phone was answered by the same female officer who had spoken to me earlier. When she recognised my voice, she gave me her news.

'DC Seymour here, sir. Inspector Wilson is just on the other line at the moment but we were about to give you a call. I've taken a good hard look at Mr and Mrs Harcourt. Did you say he told you he was a lieutenant colonel in the army?'

'In the Grenadier Guards, is what he said. He even has a tattoo to prove it.'

'Well, he was lying. He was a corporal in the Paratroop Regiment until he was given a dishonourable discharge in April 2002. I've asked the MoD for details but nothing's been forthcoming so far.'

Suddenly, the unusual parachute wings logo was explained, as was the fact that it had looked a good bit older than the Guards tattoo. I had a strong suspicion that it would turn out to be the insignia of his original regiment.

DC Seymour carried on. 'Since then, Harcourt has had no

recorded occupation although a check with his bank reveals regular payments, sizable ones, coming through the Isle of Man but originating in the Bahamas. He's never been investigated by the fraud squad but Inspector Wilson has passed on his details to them this afternoon because we reckon he might be of interest to them.'

I took a moment or two to absorb this new information. If Harcourt was prepared to lie about his true background and even go to the extent of getting himself a fictitious tattoo, then we definitely needed to take everything he had told us with a pinch of salt. 'Well, well, well, that *is* interesting. I wonder who his mysterious benefactor is and, more importantly, what he has to do in return for his money.' I also remembered that Vico Carnevale, the murderer of the Albanian drug baron who had started all this off, had been apprehended at Gatwick en route to none other than the Bahamas. I've never liked coincidences but in this case, it was starting to make sense.

DC Seymour continued. 'Nothing much known about his wife, except that her name isn't really Fleur. She was christened Flora but adopted the name Fleur after her marriage. I suppose she thought it sounded posher. Married in 2003 and no employment since then. Previously, she worked in a burger bar in Bermondsey. Ah, just a minute, Inspector Wilson's come off the phone. I'll pass you over to him.' I thanked her for her assistance and then heard Paul's voice.

'Hi, Dan. Has Seymour filled you in on the dodgy English couple?'

'Hi, Paul, yes, thanks. Very interesting.'

'How's the investigation going?'

'It's getting more and more fascinating by the minute. I'm afraid I'm on the scrounge again. Does the name Jeremy or Jezza Smith ring any bells with you?'

'Not immediately.' I heard his fingers on a keyboard. 'Hang on a minute and I'll look. Oh yes, I see he's been inside a couple of times: drugs and GBH. Looks like a right villain.'

'Thanks for that; we've already received a report on him from your people, but it mentions he's currently under suspicion in an ongoing drugs investigation. Any chance you could give one of your buddies in the drug squad a call and see if there might be anything significant there? In particular anything to link him with the drug ring we smashed three years ago in Peckham. Remember that one?'

'An Albanian guy was murdered and a guy with an Italian name was put away for it, if I remember right.'

'Dead right, Vico Carnevale, and the woman whose father has employed me to look into the death of Joseph Beck is none other than Bianca Moretti.'

'The good-looking brunette with a degree in modern languages from Oxford. I certainly remember her. Well, well, it's a small world.'

'It certainly is. Could you do me another favour, now I come to think of it? Please could you check what Bianca Moretti has been doing since coming out of prison? She told me she's a post-grad student at King's but I'd like confirmation just to be on the safe side. Realistically, we've only got until first thing tomorrow morning before three of our main suspects disappear, so anything, even just an odd snippet of information, would be greatly appreciated.'

I added my apologies for the extra hassle and thanked him most warmly. After the call had ended, I stood there, holding my phone, thinking about what he'd just said. I had remembered that Bianca had a degree but I hadn't remembered that it had been from the same university attended by Beck. For a moment, I wondered if she might have met him there, but then immediately remembered that she was just thirty-six and he had been ten years older so he would have moved on long before she started there. The other link, of course, might be that, seeing as two years ago she had been involved with a drug ring and, according to the man at MI6, Beck had been investigating another drug ring before his death, might this mean that she was involved with drugs all over again? The waters were getting muddier and muddier.

Oscar had been very patient today so as a reward, I took him to the ice-cream shop and bought him another apple-flavoured lolly. As before, this disappeared down his throat long before it even started to melt and I was then treated to loud slurping noises from behind me all the way back up the road to the Retreat as he licked his lips. I drove into Leo's car park and was pleased to see that the pickup was still there although there was no sign of his other vehicle, which he had told me he had lent to his daughter. Hopefully, she would arrive soon.

I let myself in and went up to the first floor. As I arrived, Leo looked up from reading my book and grinned. 'Where do you get your ideas from, Dan? A murderer hiding up a tree and a body in an olive press? Are you sure your years as a policeman haven't scarred you for life?'

I found myself grinning back at him, although I knew I was about to change the mood in the room with my questions. 'Just the products of my imagination. That's all.' While Oscar trotted over to be petted by him, I took a seat on the sofa opposite him and got straight to the point.

'Listen, Leo, I need to ask you something.'

He must have picked up on my tone and I saw his expression immediately change to something more serious – apprehensive maybe?

'Sure, anything.'

'When I asked you if Bianca knew Joseph Beck well, you said no. I've been listening to a number of people and I now need to ask you whether you want to reconsider your answer. Think hard. Were he and Bianca an item?'

Yet again, I saw that momentary flash of what could well have been guilt cross his face but, just as before, he then shook his head resolutely. 'No, like I said, they hardly knew each other. Hell, I probably knew him better than she did.'

It was a good try, but I knew him pretty well by now and I felt sure he wasn't telling me the whole truth so I had one more go. 'I've just come from the *questura*. The inspector has just received information that might well link Bianca to a major drugs investigation. If that's true, it could mean that she's involved with some very unpleasant people, the sort of people who think nothing of committing murder.' I added a bit of extra emphasis. 'The sort of people who can order other people to commit murder.'

An expression of horror spread across his face and I had to admit that he was either a very good actor or it had to be genuine. 'Are you trying to say that my Bianca killed Joe Beck? Man, that's impossible. Yeah, she doesn't pick her men too well; yeah, she got herself involved with some bad stuff over there in England, but that's all done now. She's paid the price and she would never, ever, be involved in murder.'

'I hear you, Leo, but you're her father and you would say that, wouldn't you?' Before he could retort, I carried on. 'What *I* think isn't important. What's important is what the inspector thinks. I'll ask you one more time before he does. Can you look me in the eye and tell me that Beck never came here? You see, it turns out from George's records that Beck left the Retreat almost every night last week at about eleven-thirty and then slipped back in again first thing in the morning. Where do you think he might have been going? My feeling is that it was here.'

He looked up from his hands and for a moment, our eyes met but then he dropped them again. 'Listen, Dan, I'm getting old and a bit deaf. I don't notice stuff as much as I used to. You'd better ask Bianca. She's a good girl. She'll tell you the truth.'

That was good enough for me. Clearly he had been ordered or begged by his daughter not to reveal her connection with Beck. He'd tried hard but he hadn't provided an outright denial and, more importantly, he hadn't brought himself to look me in the eye when he was speaking. I genuinely liked Leo and I could see that he was caught between a rock and a hard place so I didn't press the point. However, unless his daughter came clean when she was spoken to, I had a feeling Inspector Luca Sartori would be more insistent. Of course, the big unknown remained that if she had been having an affair with Beck, why could she possibly have wanted to kill him?

And if so, why involve me?

I changed the subject – well, sort of. 'Have you heard from Bianca? When's she coming back?'

'She called just before you got in. Something came up but she said she should be back just after five.'

'Would you give me a call when she arrives, please? I need to talk to her urgently.'

I checked my watch and saw that it wasn't quite four o'clock, so I told Leo I was going to take Oscar for a walk. Outside, it was still very hot so, just like before, we had a quick stroll in the scrub and then I took him to the pool again so both of us could cool down. I waved at Billy, now sheltering under a faded Martini parasol until his red one was returned from the lab, and the thought occurred to me that I hadn't heard yet what results, if any, they might have been able to get off the original. DNA from one of our prime suspects would have been good but the fact that Luca hadn't said anything made that appear a forlorn hope.

After a short splash around, Oscar and I went back up to the bar and I sat down at my usual table. I pulled my phone out of my replacement plastic bag and immediately saw that I'd received a text from Anna. In spite of the heat, I felt a chill go down my spine as I read it.

When you feel you can find time to come back and talk to me, please let me know.

I sat there helplessly for several minutes, wondering how to reply to something as terse as this, before common sense kicked in and I knew I had no option. I sent her a similarly short reply.

You're right. We need to talk. I'll come back tonight. I probably won't be there until around midnight and I'll come straight to your place. I'll text you when I'm halfway.

I had no choice. This was potentially my whole future happiness hanging in the balance and, however much I wanted to see a conclusion to this investigation, I owed it to her – and to myself – to get my priorities right.

20

FRIDAY LATE AFTERNOON

I didn't have long to dwell on this before Sophie appeared at my side and she was looking and sounding animated. 'Dan, I was hoping to see you or the inspector. I've just remembered who was on the table by the French couple on Wednesday evening when Mr Griffiths said that thing about murder. It was that German man, Mr Schinken.'

'Thanks a lot. That's great.' I tried not to sound too excited. 'I don't suppose you could remember who was on the table on the other side of Griffiths, can you? Didn't you say they might have been able to hear as well?'

'It was a couple and the more I think about it, I'm almost certain it might have been the Harcourts.' She caught my eye. 'But I couldn't swear to it in a court of law. I'm pretty sure it was them and I reckon they might well have been able to hear what was said. I'm sorry I can't be more definite, but it's just that I was so busy.' She straightened up and returned to her waitress persona. 'A cold beer and a bowl of water?'

'That sounds great, but make it a low-alcohol beer, would you? I have to drive to Florence tonight.'

'Ugh, that's a long drive. Still, it's a lovely city, isn't it?'

As soon as she'd gone off, I called Luca to pass on what Sophie had said and what Leo hadn't said but might have implied. I also passed on the information that Bianca was due back at just after five and that Leo had promised to call me when she appeared. Luca told me he and Rossi would be on their way up almost immediately and if Bianca hadn't returned, they would start the third interviews with the other main suspects, Smith, Dolcedo, Schinken and Harcourt.

After Oscar and I had both had a refreshing drink, I went back to the tower, took a shower and changed into fresh clothes. If I was going back to see Anna tonight, the least I could do was to try and look presentable. I threw all my stuff into my bag and took it down to the van so I would be ready to make a quick departure as soon as we'd finished the next round of interviews. I just hoped against hope that we would have caught our killer by then. My phone bleeped but it wasn't Anna; it was a brief text from Paul.

Sorry, nothing new on Smith. Drugs say he might be a small-time pusher but probably nothing more. Checking why Harcourt was chucked out of the army. Watch this space.

I left Leo still sitting on the sofa in the same position and went over to the Retreat. There were two squad cars in the car park and I found Sergeant Rossi at the door of the clubhouse. He beckoned me over when he saw me. 'We've just had another session with Dario Dolcedo but without any appreciable results. He still swears blind his wife wasn't cheating and, even if she had been, his faith would prevent him from doing anything as sinful as committing murder.' He shrugged his shoulders. 'I have to admit he sounded pretty convincing.'

I nodded in agreement. 'Who's next on the list?'

'The English guy, Smith.'

Luca was using Giorgio's office again and he had gone out of his way to set the scene so as to make it appear as official and threatening as possible. Officer Pellegrino, looking stern, was sitting to one side with a pad, there was a recorder on the desk and another officer standing guard by the door. Rossi and I sat down on either side of the inspector and when Jeremy Smith came in and sat down across the desk from us, I definitely felt I could detect increased nervousness on his face this time. As agreed with Luca, I did most of the talking and then provided a running translation of the interview for the Italian officers.

'Good afternoon, Mr Smith, or would you prefer me to call you Jezza?'

A little flicker of uncertainty flashed across his face.

'So tell us, which would you recommend: Belmarsh prison or Brixton?'

Any last residual traces of his cockiness evaporated and a resigned expression appeared on his face. 'I was afraid of this. You've checked my record and you've seen that I've done time, but that doesn't make me a murderer.' He looked up confrontationally. 'All right, so I've stepped out of line a few times, but I've never killed anybody and I never would.'

Still fixing him with my steely eye and keeping my tone hard, I continued. 'I'm not sure the Jamaican gentleman you beat to a pulp would agree with you. By the look of your file, you were lucky to get away with GBH and not attempted murder.' He dropped his head and I hit him with the real questions. 'Why did you bring Lorraine with you, Jezza? Was she your accomplice? Did you need a woman to act as a temptress to lure your victims to their deaths?'

His face lost its rosy pink glow as the blood drained away

from his cheeks. 'No, no, no, nothing like that. She wanted a bit of a break and so did I, so we came here together for a bit of fun. That's all.'

'And your idea of fun is bludgeoning two innocent men to death?'

'No, for God's sake, I've never done anything like that and I never would.'

'Talk to us about drugs, Jezza. Who are you involved with now? You realise that it's going to look very bad for you if you get caught dealing again.'

He looked quite shocked. 'I'm not dealing, I promise. Yes, I like a smoke every now and then, but who doesn't? Yes, there's people at the club who probably are dealing, but I'm not part of it. I'm really not.'

He sounded credible but I kept up the pressure. 'You see, the people who deal in drugs are very unpleasant people, the sort of people who kill other people. They might even kill you.'

'Why me? I haven't done anything.' His voice sounded quite plaintive now.

'Why *not* you?'

Luca and I continued questioning him for several minutes and by the time he finally left the room, I got the feeling we had frightened the life out of him. Hopefully, this might even do him some good, but I wasn't holding my breath.

As the door closed behind him, I looked across at the inspector.

'What do you think?'

'I'm not convinced he's innocent, but I'm not convinced he's guilty. He sounded pretty genuine in his denials, I'll give him that. The fact is, however, his record speaks for itself: involvement with drugs, violent behaviour, who knows? He might have been sent here to kill Beck in spite of his denials. I'm tempted to arrest him and stick him in a cell for the night. That might crystallise his thinking.'

I tended to agree with the inspector, although I was feeling a bit less sure than before that Smith was our man after all. Apart from anything else, the problem we had would be to prove his guilt – or indeed that of any of the others. So far, we had no concrete proof against anybody. I queried the lifeguard's red umbrella results and the sergeant shook his head.

'The bloodstains have definitely been identified as belonging to the first victim but there were no traces of DNA.'

'And the two whisky bottles were both wiped clean?'

'Just like the steel bars.'

The next interviewee was Klaus Schinken and he arrived, once again, with a relaxed smile on his face. This lasted only until my first question.

'We understand that you were an officer of the Stasi until 1988. Is that correct?'

Not only his face but his whole manner underwent a transformation. He appeared to shrink before our eyes and the jovial air disappeared in a flash, to be replaced by a hunted look. He had to clear his throat several times before he managed to produce a reply.

'Yes, but I only held a junior rank.'

'So you just followed orders?' I allowed a deliberate sneer to enter my voice. Now that he was visibly rattled, I wanted to keep him that way. 'Anything you were told to do, you did, right?'

He nodded. 'Yes, of course, I had to.'

'And did that include firing at unarmed civilians?'

For a moment, he looked genuinely surprised. 'Firing? You mean with a weapon? I've never fired at anybody in my life.'

'You never worked as a border guard?'

'No, I was based in Dresden. That's a long way from the border.'

'What did you do in Dresden?'

Sweat was running down his face by now. 'Records, I worked in records. You know, copying, filing, that sort of thing.'

'Does the name Heinrich Beck mean anything to you?'

He looked blank. 'No, should it?' A glimmer of comprehension appeared on his face. 'Wait a minute, the man who was killed on Saturday night was called Beck, wasn't he? Is that who you mean? But I've heard people here referring to him as Joseph.'

He sounded believable but I had to remind myself that, for all I knew, I might be sitting opposite a trained Stasi interrogator and torturer. No doubt if that had been his role, he would have picked up a lot of expertise, so I tried again.

'Heinrich Beck was the father of the man who was murdered here on Saturday night. With his wife and his son, Josef, he lived in what at the time was called Karl-Marx-Stadt. He was beaten to death by your previous employers in 1987 and his wife was then shot and killed by border guards as she and the boy tried to escape to the West. Are you sure you've never heard that name?'

He wiped his hands across his sweaty face and shook his head rapidly from side to side. 'No, never. Like I say, I spent all my time in Dresden. I wasn't involved in anything like that. If I had been, I would have remembered, but I wasn't, you have to believe me.'

We carried on questioning him until he was a pathetic mess. Bullying a sixty-five-year-old wasn't something I enjoyed doing, but I had little sympathy for anybody who had belonged to the infamous Stasi. Finally, after almost twenty minutes, Luca released him. He waited until the door had closed behind the German before turning towards me.

'What did you think?'

'I don't know what to think. He sounded credible, but then so did Smith.'

At that moment, my phone started ringing. It was Leo at the tower.

'Bianca's back.'

21

FRIDAY LATE AFTERNOON

Luca decided to delay interviewing Mr and Mrs Harcourt until after we'd spoken to Bianca. Hopefully, by that time I might have heard back from London about the reason for Oliver Harcourt's ejection from the army. The three of us left the Retreat and walked up to the tower. Just on the other side of my van, I spotted the rear of a silver Mercedes. Evidently, Bianca had brought her father's car back. We went inside and I led the two police officers up to the first floor. Bianca and her father were sitting side by side on one of the sofas, looking serious. Oscar trotted over to say hello to the two of them and this even produced a hint of a smile from Bianca, although her father was looking tense. As the interview was to be conducted in Italian, Luca did most of the questioning while Rossi took notes. I sat back and listened in.

'Your name is Bianca Moretti?' She nodded and he continued. 'I'm going to record this interview so I would advise you to think very carefully about all the answers you give.' She merely shrugged in acknowledgement and he set the recorder on the coffee table between us and pressed the record button. 'Bianca Moretti, you live in England, is that right?'

'Yes, it is.'

'Please tell me how long you've been staying here with your father.'

'Just over two weeks. I've been away for a couple of nights this week but otherwise, I've been here all the time.' Her Italian was faultless – a lot better than mine – and her tone was unruffled. She sounded completely under control.

Luca transferred his attention momentarily to her father. 'Can you confirm that, Signor Moretti?'

'I can.' His voice sounded strained and I saw Bianca reach over and catch hold of his hand in one of hers as the inspector returned to questioning her again.

'So, Signora Moretti, you were living here with your father last week and you were here on Saturday night when Joseph Beck was murdered?'

'That's correct.' Still no hint of nerves.

'Tell me, please, were you in a relationship with the victim?'

She shook her head. 'No, we spoke a few times, but there was nothing going on between us.'

Luca addressed her father. 'Can you confirm that as well, please, Signor Moretti?'

He cleared his throat and answered. 'I can.'

I definitely heard a tremor of something in his voice and I felt sure the inspector would have heard it as well. The daughter might be doing a good job of looking and sounding totally open and above board but her father clearly wasn't such an expert liar. Luca tried again, deliberately putting Leo on the spot. 'Signor Moretti, I must remind you that this is a murder investigation and lying to the police is a very serious matter. Are you absolutely sure that what you're telling us is 100 per cent true?'

Bianca cut in to answer for her father. 'My father means what he says but, in fairness, he has no way of knowing all about my personal life. I could have been having a relationship with the victim without my father knowing anything about it.' I saw her look directly at the inspector. 'But I wasn't. For the avoidance of doubt, I wasn't in any kind of relationship with Joseph Beck.'

Maybe it was just wishful thinking on my part or maybe it was just one of my old copper's hunches, but for a second, a fraction of a second, I thought I caught something in her voice when she mentioned the victim's name. I was still debating exactly what I thought I'd heard when Oscar, who had been lying happily on the cool floor, pulled himself to his feet and went over to sit beside her. He laid his big, hairy head on her knee and gazed up at her adoringly. It could be he just wanted her to stroke his ears some more, but normally when he does that sort of thing, it's because he reckons somebody is unhappy and he feels he should offer a bit of canine support. Could it be that my four-legged friend was developing into a lie detector? Did my dog believe that Bianca really had been fond of Joseph Beck? I almost smiled at the thought of telling this to a judge in a court of law. They would probably have confined me to a secure unit for my own good.

Luca carried on. 'I'm surprised to hear you say that, Signora Moretti, seeing as various people at the Retreat have told me the opposite.'

She continued to look unfazed. 'People are free to think what they like, Inspector, but surely only I know the truth about my relationships.'

Luca had another couple of tries to get her to acknowledge that she and the victim had been close, querying where he might have spent the nights when he had left the Retreat but, just like two years ago, she stonewalled every question. He referred back to her conviction in the drugs case in London and she freely accepted that she had been at fault but insisted that she was no longer involved with any of those people and had nothing to do with drugs. The inspector asked her if she would have any objection if the sergeant searched her belongings – although from what I'd seen of the spartan interior of her room, that was likely to produce absolutely nothing – she agreed immediately and Leo went upstairs with Rossi to show him the way. While her father was out of the room, I took the opportunity to ask Bianca a question of my own.

'On the occasions when you did exchange a word or two with the victim, did he ever mention what he did for a living?'

'I didn't really know him well enough to have that sort of conversation.' She sounded completely convincing. 'It was really just hello, goodbye, lovely weather. That sort of thing.'

'If I were to tell you that he worked for the British security services, would that come as a surprise?'

She dropped her eyes and transferred her attention to Oscar, who was still glued to her. She stroked his ears and answered without looking up. 'I don't think I've ever met anybody from the security services. I suppose anybody could be, really.' She finally looked up and there was a twinkle in her eye. 'Why, even you, Dan, might be a spy and I'd never have guessed.'

We carried on firing questions at her but came out of it none the wiser. Just like two years earlier, I couldn't shift the suspicion that she knew a whole lot more than she was giving away, but it was clear that she had told us everything she intended to tell us and nothing more. When Sergeant Rossi followed Leo back downstairs again, shaking his head, Luca stood up and I followed his example.

'Thank you, Signora Moretti, you will be hearing from us again.' He turned off the voice recorder and the three of us went down the stairs and outside into the late-afternoon sunshine. Luca waited until we were almost down at the gate before stopping and glancing back up towards the tower. 'She's like a block of ice, isn't she? It's very rare to meet anybody quite as expression-less. I don't know about you, Dan, but I still have a very strong feeling that there *was* something going on between her and Beck, but I have an equally strong feeling that she's not going to talk. She's either very frightened or totally committed. Is that the impression you got?'

'That's exactly what I think. Of course, the big question still remains: assuming for a moment that she was in a relationship with the victim, does this mean she killed him and, if so, why did she do it? What could possibly make love change to loathing at the drop of a hat? This isn't *Othello*, after all.'

We both looked across at Rossi, who shrugged his shoulders. 'Quite inscrutable, and her belongings were the bare minimum. She reminds me of that Chinese guy we picked up two years ago with a sack full of body parts in the boot of his car. Try as we could, he just sat there and denied any involvement. That's what it felt like with Signora Moretti. Like trying to get blood out of a stone.'

Luca nodded. 'Although she's told us nothing, to my mind this lack of response only increases her possible guilt. Most normal people in a murder inquiry show a whole lot more emotion. Like her father, for example. To back her up, he was lying, and I'm sure all three of us saw it on his face, but his daughter? Nothing. Anyway, she's definitely staying on the list of prime suspects. Somebody as cold and calculating as that could well be a murderer although, like you Dan, I still can't think why she might have done it.'

My phone bleeped and I was delighted to see that it was a message from Paul.

Bianca Moretti definitely a postgrad at King's. Self-funded and report-edly doing very well. Corporal Oliver Harcourt was chucked out of the army for potential war crimes, abusing, torturing and killing Afghan prisoners. All hushed up. Hope this helps.

It certainly did. I was pleased to hear that Bianca had been telling the truth about her studies, and the fact that she was paying her own way came as no surprise. Maybe this was with remnants of the drug profits from two years ago or, if not, I felt sure her father would be subsidising her. In spite of her criminal past, I was still reluctant to believe that she could have been involved in anything as awful as murder, but there was no getting away from the fact that she still wasn't telling us everything. No doubt Luca would be interviewing her again, maybe down at the police station, and that might loosen her tongue. However, as far as Harcourt was concerned, this information definitely added another nail to his coffin. By the sound of it, he was a proven killer and a sadist to boot. Exactly the kind of person who might have bludgeoned Beck to death and then killed a harmless Welshman just in case.

Back at the Retreat, we took up our places again in Giorgio's office and Oliver Harcourt was summoned. He came in looking relatively untroubled with that same supercilious air that he and his wife had demonstrated before. Interestingly, even though I now knew that he wasn't a haughty, upper-class snob, I still disliked him. Maybe it wasn't a class thing after all. Just like Oscar can sniff one dog's butt and start wagging his tail and then sniff another, raise his hackles and take two steps backwards, that was my reaction to seeing Harcourt again. There was something about this guy that just stank. I went onto the offensive straight away.

'We would be interested to know, Mr Harcourt, how you managed to achieve lightning promotion from corporal to lieutenant colonel even though you had been thrown out of the army. Would you care to explain?'

The man froze and his haughty persona morphed instantly into something far shiftier. 'What do you mean? I don't understand...' He was flapping about helplessly.

'Were you or were you not in the Parachute Regiment?' A check on the Internet a few minutes earlier had revealed that the insignia of that regiment was a pair of wings with a crown above it and this tattoo was exactly what was now staring me in the face.

'Erm, yes.'

'And was your departure from the regiment in 2002 your own choice or were you kicked out?' I could see him desperately trying to think of a way out of the predicament in which he now found himself but I had no sympathy. 'Abusing, torturing and killing prisoners, that's not very nice.'

His face, which had been getting redder, now became positively puce. 'How do you know that? That's classified information. Besides, no charges were ever brought against me. It was my word against a bunch of murderous scum.'

'And your superior officers believed the murderous scum rather than Corporal Harcourt. You must have been very unhappy about that.'

He dropped his eyes and made no attempt to reply but I distinctly heard him murmur the word, 'Bastards.'

I assumed he was referring to the people who had kicked him out of the army, but he might have been talking about us. Either way, he was now quite clearly shocked and upset and, hopefully, sufficiently vulnerable to start answering our questions honestly.

'Tell us about the large payments you receive from the Bahamas.'

An expression of terror crossed his face and he literally jumped a few inches and when he looked up, we could see disbelief in his eyes.

'How do you know that? That's personal, that's private.'

I was determined not to let him off the hook. 'There's nothing personal and private in a murder investigation. Would I be right in thinking that you developed a taste for hurting and killing people when you were in the army and you've been carrying on doing just that since you left – for a price? What's the going rate for murder these days, Corporal?'

'I don't... I don't know what you mean.' I saw him make a weak attempt to look offended. 'That's slander. I could sue you for saying things like that.'

I ignored the empty threat. 'The inspector would like to know who sent you here to murder Joseph Beck.'

'What? Me, murder? Never.' He was now doing a better job of trying to sound outraged but, to my ear, he was playacting. Interestingly, even though he was visibly in an emotional state, Oscar made no attempt to get up and go over to offer support. Heartened by my dog's vote of no confidence, I pressed home my advantage.

'What about your wife, Oliver? Was she in on it with you?'

'No, of course not.' He was clearly floundering.

'You want us to believe that you managed to kill two people without your wife seeing, hearing or suspecting anything? What sort of idiots do you take us for? We're going to haul her in here now and ask her all about it. I wouldn't mind betting that the two of you work as a team. After all, where else did she think the money came from that allowed you to buy yourselves a swanky house and join the local golf club?'

Presumably, his military training must have finally started to kick in again by now and I saw him take a few deep breaths. 'If you must know, the money comes from investments. I'm not a murderer and I resent the accusation.'

This was a better attempt, but it still didn't convince me, and I felt pretty sure it wouldn't convince Luca either. We continued questioning him, trying to tie down his movements on the nights of the murders, but he continued to deny any involvement. Finally, Luca gave instructions to the officer at the door to send the wife in. Rossi and Pellegrino accompanied Harcourt out of the room with strict instructions that he wasn't to communicate with his wife in any way.

She appeared a minute later in a state of high dudgeon, positively bristling with indignation. 'What on earth is going on? Why am I being summoned like a criminal? It's quite simply unbearable.' She had adopted her fruitiest accent.

Luca waved her into the seat recently occupied by her husband and waited until the other two officers came back before making a start. I translated for him as he went straight for the jugular. 'Tell me, Mrs Harcourt, when was it that you discovered that your husband was a killer? Was it before or after you gave up your job in the burger bar?'

Her jaw literally dropped and her mouth gaped open in astonishment. She gave no immediate response but that might just have been because she was still struggling for air. Luca didn't give her time to settle.

'Your husband was sent here to kill Joseph Beck.' He didn't phrase it as a question and I did my best to reproduce his deadpan tone when I translated. I watched the expression on her face as the accusation registered. Her reaction was a fascinating sequence of expressions, starting with shock, moving clearly into dismay, and then, belatedly, changing to outrage.

'I've never heard such a load of old rubbish in all my life.'

Interestingly, her accent and vocabulary were slipping from *Downton Abbey* to *Eastenders*.

'Are you saying you didn't work in a burger bar?'

'No... yes, I mean, that's irrelevant. What I object to is you insinuating that Oliver is a murderer. Who do you think you are?'

Luca was doing a great job. He answered in almost cordial tones but with a wonderful undercurrent of menace. 'Now that's a good question. I'm a police officer, but who do *you* think you are?'

'My name is Fleur Harcourt, Mrs Fleur Harcourt. You know that full well.'

Still sounding urbane, Luca continued the attack and I did my best to echo his tone in my translation. 'I put it to you, Flora...' I laid special emphasis on her real name as Luca had done '...that you and your husband have set up a profitable little business doing other people's dirty work. What I'd like to know is who sent you here to kill Joseph Beck.'

'That's ridiculous. Of course we didn't come here to kill anybody. We're on holiday and we've done nothing wrong. I trust that, even though we're in Italy, the law here still says that all people are innocent until proved guilty.' She looked across at us and there was real hatred in her eyes. 'But you have no proof, so I suggest you look elsewhere for your murderer.' She jumped to her feet and this time, there was an infuriating spark of triumph in her eyes. 'Proof, you stupid people, you need proof and you don't have any.'

With that, she turned and stomped towards the door. The constable stayed where he was and barred her way while he looked across at the inspector, who hesitated for a moment and then nodded to him. The officer stepped aside and Flora, AKA Fleur Harcourt, stormed out.

22

FRIDAY EARLY EVENING

After the door had closed behind Mrs Harcourt, we all looked at each other. Luca spoke first. 'I think I can safely say that those two were made for each other. A most unpleasant couple of people, but are they killers?'

I answered first. 'The way I see it, we have three suspects here with potential motive. This last couple who were sent as hired killers, Smith and his girlfriend who might be involved with a drug racket and may also have been sent to eliminate Beck, who'd been sticking his nose too far into their business, but there's also the German. Klaus Schinken is the right age and the right nationality and he comes from around the right area to have been involved in the deaths of Beck's mother and father, and it could be he committed murder to protect his reputation.'

Luca nodded in agreement. 'And what about Bianca Moretti? Should we include her on the list? Rossi, what do you think?'

He nodded slowly. 'Unlike any of the others, she was just so unmoved, so apparently untroubled, that I wouldn't rule her out yet. I found her lack of emotion quite unsettling.'

Luca turned towards the female officer. 'What about you,

Pellegrino? Did any of the people we've interviewed this afternoon strike you as killers?'

The constable looked pleased to have been included. 'I wasn't there to hear what Bianca Moretti said but, of the ones we've seen here, I definitely feel that this last couple are the most likely.'

Luca turned back towards me. 'What's your verdict, Dan?'

I didn't have to give it much thought. 'Fascinating as the German connection might be, I really didn't get the impression that Schinken would have had the guts to commit one, let alone two, brutal murders. Bianca Moretti is undeniably a cold fish but, again, I don't see her as a killer and I'm at a loss to come up with a viable motive for her. Jezza Smith might well be capable of murder, but I tended to believe his story so, of all of them, I agree with Officer Pellegrino and my choice would be the former Corporal Harcourt, aided and abetted by his wife.'

Luca nodded several times. 'My feelings entirely but, like the charming Mrs Harcourt just told us, we need proof and we have none. Yes, he's been lying about his military service and rank, but that's hardly proof that he's a killer. The more I look at both murders, the more they appear to be the work of professionals. In fact, if it hadn't been for Bianca Moretti, Beck's murder would almost have been forgotten by now, just an unfortunate accident. Both were professional hits and I agree that the most likely perpetrator is Oliver Harcourt, almost certainly with the assistance of his wife. But do I have enough to arrest them? If not, then they're going to leave here tomorrow and that will be pretty much my last chance of nailing them.' He gave a frustrated sigh and stood up. 'Come on, I could do with a coffee.'

We all trooped out to the bar and sat down around a table. Many of the other tables were occupied and I noticed Jezza Smith and Lorraine on one and Oliver and Fleur Harcourt on another. I couldn't see Klaus Schinken but he had probably gone off for a lie-down after his earlier grilling. We ordered our drinks – I had a double espresso to help keep me awake on my drive back to Florence – and silence settled on the table. For a moment or two, I caught the eye of Mrs Harcourt and the smug insolence of it made my skin creep. Her husband had what looked like a glass of brandy on the table in front of him alongside a plastic bag presumably containing his valuables. Evidently I was not alone in finding a use for a shopping bag. There was an empty glass near it so it looked as though he had felt in need of alcoholic support. As my eyes alighted on his plastic bag, it looked vaguely familiar and a thought occurred to me. Could it be? I looked across at Sergeant Rossi.

'When your people searched the accommodation belonging to the suspects, did they check their wallets and phones? I think we should check everything, however insignificant, for Mr and Mrs Harcourt and maybe Jeremy Smith and his girlfriend as well.'

The sergeant glanced across at his boss, who nodded. 'Phones, yes, but not wallets as far as I know. Good idea. Go and collect them now, Rossi, and we'll take a look.'

A minute later, there were four bags on the table in front of us: two women's handbags, a leather pouch belonging to Smith and the plastic bag belonging to Oliver Harcourt. My eyes lit up when I saw it. It was exactly what I'd thought I'd recognised and my eyes were drawn to the writing on the outside: *Gatwick Duty Free*. From the size of it, a couple of bottles of Johnnie Walker Red Label would have fitted in it quite comfortably. I tipped the contents onto the table and sifted through, looking in vain for any clue until I reached his wallet. This contained the usual credit cards, driving licence and several hundred euros in cash as well as a sheaf of receipts. Here in Italy, in an attempt to cut down on the black economy, the Italian government introduced a law quite a few years ago obliging all shop owners and other merchants to provide a printed receipt for every transaction. The result of this is that my pockets tend to get full of scrap paper very quickly. Maybe if I drank a bit less coffee and beer... I flicked through the receipts until I suddenly struck gold. I pulled one out of the pile and passed it across to Luca.

'That was very sloppy of them. Take a look at that: two bottles of Johnnie Walker Red Label bought at the duty-free shop in London. That should give you enough proof to arrest both of them and hold them while you do an in-depth study of bank and phone records. I think we might have a couple of professional killers on our hands. If you like, I can have a word with my friend at the Metropolitan Police and ask him to get somebody to do a careful check of unsolved suspicious deaths in the UK over the last twenty years or so, carried out by a murderer who leaves virtually no clues. I'll ask London to see if any of those murders match up with the regular deposits of large sums in the Harcourt account. Hopefully, they can cross-reference payments and deaths with stamps in his passport in the case of any hits that took place overseas.' Although this would involve a lot more work for Paul and his colleagues, if it led to the resolution of a series of unsolved murders, I felt sure it would do his career no harm at all. Putting this couple his way was the least I could do after all the help I'd had from him.

Luca reached over and clapped me on the back. 'Brilliant, Dan, do that, please.' He was grinning from ear to ear. 'You're right, with this little piece of paper we've got Harcourt. I'm sure the *pubblico ministero* will be happy to go ahead with charges.' There was considerable satisfaction on his face and he gave instructions to his officers. 'Rossi, Pellegrino, arrest Mr and Mrs Harcourt on suspicion of murder. Take them to the *questura* – two cars, no conferring.' He turned back towards me and gave me a broad smile. 'Thanks, Dan, for all your help. I couldn't have done it without you.'

'I don't believe it. You were doing fine. I just got lucky at the end.'

'Can I at least take you out for a good meal tonight? That's the least you deserve.'

I shook my head regretfully. 'That's a very kind offer, Luca, but I have to get back to Florence tonight. I'm in the doghouse with my girlfriend and I need to try and sort things out. In fact, I need to leave as soon as possible.'

'Didn't you say you were coming back to Alassio in a couple of weeks to celebrate your birthday? We'll do it then.'

I thanked him for the offer, but I had a sinking feeling that I might not be coming back in two weeks' time or, at least, not with Anna.

After making a long call to London and passing on Paul's contact details to Luca so his people could send on all the relevant information from this end, I stood up and we shook hands. Hopefully unmasking the Harcourts would look very good on both their records. He wished me *buon viaggio* and I asked him to say goodbye to his officers for me, with whom I'd been very impressed. Leaving him there to finish off, I went inside to say goodbye to the staff. After receiving hugs from two naked women and a naked – and very hirsute – man, I led Oscar back out of the gate for the last time, stopping briefly at the checkpoint to speak to Dario.

'Dario, I'm leaving now. I'm sorry the last couple of days have been tough for you, but the good news is that the inspector has caught the killer.'

An expression of profound relief crossed his face and he reached out and pumped my hand in both of his. 'Thank you so much. It's been a worrying time, but I'm so glad you've caught the killer. Are you allowed to tell me who it was?'

Just at that moment, two police cars emerged from the car park and drove past us. As they did so, the faces of Oliver and Fleur Harcourt were clearly visible on the back seats, one in each vehicle. I waited until they had passed before giving Dario a wink. 'See if you can guess.'

Before going back to the tower to return Leo's keys and to give him and his daughter the good news, I took Oscar for a walk along the headland so he could stretch his legs before the long drive home. Although the road ahead of me promised to be hard going, I couldn't complain about the weather. It was a delightful evening and the good news was that as I was going east, I would have the sun behind me, rather than in my eyes. I stood and admired the view one last time, watching a pair of speedboats racing each other across the glassy surface of the Ligurian Sea. It was a charming view and I found myself hoping that the next time I saw it, Anna would be at my side. But would she be?

Back at the tower, I let myself in and went up to the first floor. Bianca and her father were still sitting in almost exactly the same position and he, in particular, was looking tense.

'*Ciao.* I've brought you back your keys, Leo. And I brought you both some very good news. The inspector has just arrested the killers.'

An expression of immense relief flooded across his face while his daughter just gave me a pleasant smile and a measured reply. She really was as cool as a cucumber. 'That's good to hear, Dan. Tell me, did the inspector really catch the killer or was it you?'

I smiled back. 'It was a team effort, Bianca.'

'Who was it?' Leo had finally managed to regain the power of speech.

'A very unpleasant English couple called Harcourt. We think

he's a professional hitman although, for all I know, she might be the brains behind it.'

'Who would send a hitman here?' Leo sounded completely bamboozled.

'Everything points towards it being connected with the drug investigation Joseph Beck was involved with. Presumably, he must have got a bit too close for comfort and the guys at the top decided to rub him out.' I glanced at Bianca and, for once, I spotted real emotion on her face so I took a chance. 'I'm sorry, Bianca. I know you'll miss him.'

I saw her swallow hard before replying. 'You *know* that, do you?'

I gave her a little smile. 'It's just a feeling I have. Anyway, thanks a lot, Leo, for your hospitality, and I'm glad you called me in. It's been a pleasure to meet you.'

He came across and gripped my hand in both of his. 'Without you, I'm sure we wouldn't have got here. Thanks a lot, buddy. Promise me next time you're in the area, you'll give me a call. There will always be a room here for you and good old Oscar. Bring your girlfriend next time.'

Bianca then surprised me by coming over and giving me a warm hug. When her mouth was very near my ear, I felt the touch of her lips on my neck and I heard her whisper, 'Thanks, Dan.'

I smiled at her. 'I hope your studies go well. All the very best to you.' And I meant it.

I was about to leave when she turned and picked up my book from the sofa. 'Would you mind signing it? That way, I can tell people I know a famous author.'

Feeling suitably embarrassed, I took a pen and signed across the title page:

To my good friends Leo and Bianca
Best wishes for the future
Dan Armstrong.

After they had both made a fuss of Oscar and Leo had carved him a huge slice of ham, I went back down to the front door. The two of them came with me and stood at the top of the steps as I settled Oscar into the back of the van. I walked around to the driver's door and, as I did so, I cast an admiring eye over Leo's car that Bianca had been driving. It was a very smart, silver, Mercedes sports car, only marred by a nasty crack in the glass of the wing mirror. As I spotted this, a blinding flash of realisation suddenly flooded my brain. The last time I had seen this car had been in a far corner of the car park of a swanky hotel on the *corniche* above Menton.

At last it all made sense: Bianca's connection with Joseph Beck was explained, as was her refusal to speak up to defend herself or to tell me any more than the bare minimum. I now knew how it was that my dinner companion from MI6 had been so well informed about the Retreat and I also realised where Bianca had been for the last two days. I wondered if she had even been sitting in the shadows somewhere watching while I had had my haute cuisine dinner with 'God' – her boss.

I toyed with the idea of saying something but decided to leave it at that. Spies live in a very secret world and they understandably value their anonymity. I gave her and her dad a wave and I drove down to the gates, which opened for me. I found myself marvelling that almost certainly this meant that the reason Bianca had steadfastly refused to speak even on her own behalf two years ago must have been because she had been so deeply undercover that she had been prepared to go to jail for the sake of her credibility in the eyes of some truly awful people. I pulled out onto the road and speeded up, hoping the drug investigation would be successfully concluded before the same thing happened to her as had happened to her boyfriend. I glanced back at Oscar, who was standing in the boot with his nose resting on the back of the seat.

'I love my job, Oscar, but I'm not sure I'd be prepared to go to jail for it. Jesus!'

I had only just finished speaking when a motorbike, travelling at a ridiculous speed, appeared around the hairpin bend in front of me, completely on my side of the road. I spun the wheel to avoid it but felt it make contact with my front wing and I smashed through an old iron gate. My last memory before I blacked out was of plunging over a near-vertical drop.

23

FRIDAY NIGHT / SATURDAY

'Dan, can you hear me?'

I was swimming through porridge. Oscar was swimming beside me but he was spending most of his time eating the porridge and this had made him start to lag behind. Behind us was darkness but ahead was light. The voice came again and I began to realise that I recognised it. With a struggle, I forced my eyelids open a couple of millimetres and I heard a sharp intake of breath. For the first time, I realised that somebody was holding my hand and that somebody was now squeezing it so tightly, it shook me out of my trance. I opened my eyes a bit more and looked up at her.

'Anna, it's you.' Not the most original three words in the English language but from the reaction on her face, they were what she'd been waiting to hear. To my delight, she leant forward and smothered my face with kisses before straightening up, tears streaming down her cheeks, her eyes locked onto mine.

'How do you feel?'

That was an interesting question. I had a pounding headache and my eyelids felt heavy, so I did a slow check of the rest of me. I was pretty obviously lying on my back in a hospital bed and the first thing I noticed was that my left arm had two different tubes sticking in it. A heart-rate monitor was connected to my upper arm and I could hear a regular bleep from somewhere just out of my sightline. I tried to move my fingers and toes and was relieved to find that they still worked. I blinked a few times and looked up into Anna's face.

'I'm fine. What are you doing here?' My voice was more of a croak.

'What do you think I'm doing, you idiot?' Her tone was kind.

The porridge in my brain was gradually beginning to clear. 'But you're in Florence...'

'Not now, I'm not, and before you ask, you're in hospital here in San Clemente.'

'But I was on my way to see you...' The porridge was taking its time to evaporate.

'So I understand, but then you took a detour down a cliff. Inspector Sartori phoned Lina and she phoned me and I drove up here to be with you.'

'But that must have taken hours.' I raised my left arm to check my watch but my wrist was bare – unless you counted a couple of bits of plastic tubing. 'What time is it?'

'It's almost midnight. They tell me you've been drifting in and out of consciousness since they brought you in some hours ago.' Her expression became more serious. 'You gave us all an awful fright.' Her smile returned. 'But you're awake now and you sound lucid – at least, as lucid as an idiot like you ever sounds.'

I reached up with my right hand and let my fingers rest against her cheek. 'And I *am* an idiot, I'm glad you know that. Listen, Anna, I've been so stupid; of course I want to be with you...'

She leant down and kissed me softly on the lips. 'Shush,

there's no need to go through all that now.' She kissed me again. 'We'll sort it out.' Then she released my hand and stood up. 'Now I have to go and tell the doctors you're awake.'

A new thought flashed through my aching head. 'Oscar? Is he all right? Tell me he's all right. If I've ended up in here, what happened to him?' The idea of something bad happening to my canine best friend actually sent an ice-cold shaft of fear through me. Anna laid a comforting hand on the arm without the pipes in it.

'He's a tough old dog. Not a mark on him. He's fine and you can see for yourself. He's waiting just outside the door.'

'They let him into the hospital?'

'I'll be back.'

Ten seconds after she left the room, the door opened again and a hairy, black face appeared, smiling from ear to ear. He was pulling so hard against the lead, he was almost throttling himself as he struggled to get across to the bed, panting like a steam train. On the other end of the lead was the now familiar figure of Inspector Luca Sartori with almost as broad a smile as my dog's.

'*Ciao*, Dan. It's good to see you with your eyes open. Oscar, I'm sorry but no! No climbing on beds. Doctor's orders.'

While Luca hung manfully onto the end of the lead, Oscar had to be content with stretching up and setting about licking my free hand as if it were his juiciest bone. I looked down at him and could see that he had emerged from the accident a whole lot better than I had. I glanced up at Luca.

'*Ciao*, Oscar, and it's good to see you too, Luca.' My voice was sounding a bit stronger now. 'Thanks for bringing my four-legged friend. How did you manage to get a dog in here?'

He shot me a wink. 'I flashed my badge and told them he was a sniffer dog, but I didn't say for what.'

'I'm sorry to drag you out at this time of night.'

He shook his head. 'No problem. By the way, Leo Moretti says he'll look after Oscar and your girlfriend – with whom I've just been having a very pleasant chat for the past half-hour – until they let you out of here.' He grinned. 'She must love you very much to have dropped everything and driven three hundred kilometres to get here.'

Memory of the accident was starting to come back to me. 'There was a motorbike. What happened to the rider?'

'He's in a bed a bit further along the corridor with two broken legs. He'll live and, hopefully, he'll learn. The good news is that he's fully insured because your van's only good for scrap now, I'm afraid.' The door behind him started to open so he patted me on the shoulder. 'That'll be the doctor. I told him I just had to check the room with my sniffer dog and then we'd leave him to it. I'll see you when you get out. How about that meal I promised you tomorrow lunchtime?'

'Thanks a lot, Luca. You're a real friend.' I reached down again and scratched my dog's ears. 'And so are you, Oscar.'

His tail, which had been wagging ever since his enthusiastic entrance, started wagging even harder.

* * *

I was released from hospital around mid-morning on Saturday. The trauma specialist checked me over and told me I appeared to be suffering no serious ill effects after the thump my head had received against the door pillar of the van after the aged airbag had failed to deploy. He told me to take it easy for a few days and not to do anything silly. I told him I had every intention of taking it very easy indeed. All the various tubes and wires were disconnected from my body and I slid gingerly out of bed. I was relieved to find that my balance appeared unimpaired and I was able to dress myself, albeit cautiously. The only trouble I had was when it came to my socks and shoes. When I bent forward, my head started swimming and I had to straighten up again and lean against the wall. Fortunately, at that moment, Anna appeared and sat me down on the bedside chair while she knelt in front of me and helped me as if I were a little child. I reached out and stroked her cheek.

'Thank you, *carissima*. I don't know what I'd do without you.'

She shot me such a warm answering smile that I almost bent down and kissed her – only concern for my aching head stopped me.

Last night my visitors – both two- and four-legged – had been shooed away by the nursing staff almost immediately after I'd woken up and I had undergone a thorough examination by two doctors. It had been well past midnight before all the tests had been completed and they had declared themselves satisfied with my condition. After that, I had subsided into a solid, six-hour sleep – probably chemically assisted – only waking when a nurse came in to check on me first thing in the morning. Anna had arrived just after breakfast, enthusing about the hospitality she had been afforded by Leo and Bianca and, finally, she and I had been able to have our heart-to-heart.

I had repeated that I was an idiot and she hadn't disagreed with me, but she'd been good enough to tell me that she fully understood my hesitation about moving in together and she had decided that it would be best to put this off for now. Belatedly, I told her I thought cohabitation was a wonderful idea and after going round and round in circles a few times, we came to a sensible compromise. It was now early June and the next three months would most probably be stiflingly hot in Florence so she would move into my little house in the hills with me, where there's always a bit of a breeze and the air's cleaner and fresher than down in the crowded, busy city. September would be the time to assess how the summer had gone and then make a decision about where to live – my place in the country or back in the city where she had a lovely apartment in a Renaissance building a stone's throw from the Ponte Vecchio. Or maybe a bit of both.

We travelled down in the lift and I took a closer look at myself in the mirror on the wall. The left side of my forehead was a spectacular violet colour but Anna told me she had heard from Luca that I'd been very lucky indeed. As the van had careered down a near vertical slope, a providential – and very sturdy – olive tree had stopped its fall, leaving it hanging precariously over a far steeper cliff. It had taken a mobile crane to lift the battered remains of the van back up the slope before the paramedics could safely remove me from the vehicle. All the time that I had been hanging there unconscious, Oscar, who had been catapulted over the back seat miraculously without injury, had remained tight against me, refusing to leave my side.

He really is a very good dog.

As it turned out, lunch was provided by Leo Moretti, ably assisted by his daughter. The other guests were Luca Sartori – still complaining that *he* should be the one offering lunch – as well as Giorgio from the Retreat, almost unrecognisable with his clothes on – and his bubbly wife, Ginny, who evidently knew Luca's wife, Barbara, well. We drank champagne and ate lobster thermidor – a first for me. Leo revealed that this had involved meticulously removing the meat from a pile of lobsters, cooking it in a rich wine sauce and then returning it to the half shells before browning it in the oven. The secret, he told us, was to mix egg yolks and brandy with a little Dijon mustard and a heap of Gruyère cheese. The result was excellent and, although I had arrived at table with little appetite, I was heartened to find that I managed to clear my plate without difficulty. On the instructions of Anna, who sat closely beside me and kept an eye on me, I limited myself to just one small glass of champagne and stuck to the mineral water for now.

As we ate, Luca gave us the latest news on the case and it came as no surprise to hear that Oliver Harcourt and his wife had been falling over themselves to shift the blame onto each other. The wife had been loudly claiming to be the hapless victim in a coercive marriage while Oliver described her as an evil witch who had bullied him to go along with her warped and twisted schemes. Whatever the truth of their respective guilt, it was clear that, between us, we had definitely apprehended the killers of Joseph Beck and Owen Griffiths – and quite possibly a long list of previous victims of these cold-blooded murderers.

At the end of the meal, after a stunning strawberry and cream soufflé with crushed meringue and home-made ice cream, I insisted that Anna should have a snooze after her frantic drive the previous night and all the stress of the aftermath of my accident, while I took my four-legged friend for a gentle walk. To my surprise, Bianca offered to accompany us, and Oscar as ever appeared delighted to have feminine company. As we walked, she told me more of the history of her father's tower and I learned that it had started life as a safe haven for inhabitants of the villages along the coast back in the Middle Ages when marauding pirates from North Africa had come on regular raids, raping, pillaging, killing or taking into slavery all those they found. More recently, it had served as a prison during Napoleonic times. When we stopped for a rest under an old thorn tree, I brought the subject back to prisons.

'What's your plan when you finish your PhD? I hope it won't involve any more visits to prison.'

She caught my eye for a moment before looking away. 'I'm still trying to make up my mind. My supervisor at King's is trying to persuade me to give university lecturing a go but I'm not completely sure that's the direction I want to go in.'

I reached across and tapped her gently on the back of the hand. 'Life is short, Bianca. Think of your friend Joseph Beck. I have a feeling you've used up quite a few of your nine lives already. If you want my advice, I'd go for academia all the way.' I waited a couple of moments and then added a little bit of weight. 'I'm sure "God" will understand.'

She looked up sharply but then, just as quickly, dropped her eyes again. It took at least a minute before she continued and, in spite of her remarkable acting skills, I could see that she was in the prey of powerful emotions.

'You worked it out. I knew you were good, but I hadn't realised how good. This means *I'm* not as good as I thought I was, so maybe you're right and it's time to get out.' She didn't wait for me to acknowledge the compliment. 'I loved Joseph. And he loved me. He gained a reputation as a serial womaniser but after we met and fell in love, all his flirting with other women was a defensive screen that he put up to protect me. He knew his life was on the line and he did everything he could to keep me safe. I know you've caught his killers but I owe it to him to nail the guys who gave the orders. I'm sure I know who they are but we still need proof.'

'It's your call, Bianca, but for my money you're already sailing too close to the wind. You don't owe it to Joseph to get yourself killed. Let somebody else wind things up. Give up the day job and make a change.' I gave her an encouraging smile. 'That's what I did and I have no regrets.' I waved in the general direction of the beach below and the bright blue of the sea beyond. 'Back in my days at Scotland Yard, I could only dream about places like this. Since moving to Italy, I've found a whole new lease of life, not to mention a wonderful partner.' There was a movement at my feet and a black nose landed on my knee. 'Make that two partners.' I fondled Oscar's ears for a few moments. 'Anyway, you're a big girl and you know your own mind, but that's the way I see it.'

She looked up at me and there was a warm smile on her face as she leant over and kissed me softly on the cheek. 'Thanks for everything, Dan. Maybe you're right. Maybe university life is what I need.' She glanced down affectionately at Oscar. 'And maybe I should get myself a Labrador.'

'Everybody should have a Labrador like Oscar.'

He just wagged his tail. He already knew that.

ACKNOWLEDGEMENTS

Warmest thanks to my lovely editor, Emily Ruston, and the whole team at my exceptional publishers, Boldwood Books, with a special mention to Sue Smith, whose eagle eye misses very little, and Emily Reader, proofreader par excellence. I am immensely grateful to the talented Simon Mattacks for reproducing the voice of Dan in the audio version so perfectly. And finally a heartfelt thank you to Cella and Guido for introducing me to Liguria and offering such wonderful hospitality. If anybody out there is looking for a warm, scenic holiday destination – with some of the best food in the world – why not give the Italian Riviera a try?

ABOUT THE AUTHOR

T. A. Williams is the author of The Armstrong and Oscar Cozy Mystery Series, cosy crime stories set in his beloved Italy, featuring the adventures of DCI Armstrong and his labrador Oscar.

Trevor lives in Devon with his Italian wife.

Sign up to T. A. Williams' mailing list here for news, competitions and updates on future books.

Visit T. A. Williams' website: http://www.tawilliamsbooks.com

Follow T. A. Williams' on social media:

x.com/TAWilliamsBooks
facebook.com/TrevorWilliamsBooks

ALSO BY T. A. WILLIAMS

The Armstrong and Oscar Cozy Mystery Series

Murder in Tuscany

Murder in Chianti

Murder in Florence

Murder in Siena

Murder at the Matterhorn

Murder at the Leaning Tower

Murder on the Italian Riviera

Poison
& Pens

POISON & PENS IS THE HOME OF
COZY MYSTERIES SO POUR YOURSELF
A CUP OF TEA & GET SLEUTHING!

DISCOVER PAGE-TURNING NOVELS FROM
YOUR FAVOURITE AUTHORS &
MEET NEW FRIENDS

JOIN OUR
FACEBOOK GROUP

BIT.LYPOISONANDPENSFB

SIGN UP TO OUR
NEWSLETTER

BIT.LY/POISONANDPENSNEWS

Boldwᴏᴏd

Boldwood Books is an award-winning fiction publishing company seeking out the best stories from around the world.

Find out more at www.boldwoodbooks.com

Join our reader community for brilliant books, competitions and offers!

Follow us
@BoldwoodBooks
@TheBoldBookClub

Sign up to our weekly deals newsletter

https://bit.ly/BoldwoodBNewsletter

Printed in Great Britain
by Amazon

42711953R00136